SPECTRE COLLECTORS

RISE OF THE GHOSTFATHER!

SPECTRE COLLECTORS

RISE OF THE GHOSTFATHER!

BARRY HUTCHISON

nosy
crow

First published 2019 by Nosy Crow Ltd
The Crow's Nest, 14 Baden Place, Crosby Row
London SE1 1YW, UK
www.nosycrow.com

ISBN: 978 1 78800 050 5

Nosy Crow and associated logos are trademarks
and/or registered trademarks of Nosy Crow Ltd

Printed and bound in the UK by Clays Ltd, Elcograf S.p.A.
Typeset by Tiger Media

Papers used by Nosy Crow are made from wood grown in
sustainable forests.

For Mia,
Creator of Tabatha and Saku.

(But, just so we're clear, no, you're
not getting paid.)

CHAPTER 1

Denzel Edgar hadn't signed up for this.

OK, technically he *had* signed up for it when he'd agreed to join the Spectre Collectors, a centuries-old secret society dedicated to protecting Earth from supernatural threats. He'd known there'd be a certain amount of "ghost stuff" involved, since that was pretty much the whole point of the organisation. He just didn't think it'd be anything like this.

Denzel sat on an uncomfortable plastic chair directly across a table from a large, semi-transparent man. The way the man was staring at him was making Denzel deeply uncomfortable. What was making him even more uncomfortable was the fact that the man was holding his detached head under one arm.

Wait. No. Not "man". Denzel silently scolded himself. "Don't think of them as men and women." That's what Boyle, one of the longer-serving Spectre Collectors had told him. "They're not people, they're ghosts."

And yet, if you ignored the fact that he was holding his head under one arm and was partly see-through, the ghost across the table looked like a man. Denzel and his fellow new-start, Smithy, had become quite vocal on the subject of ghost rights since joining up. Granted, this was mostly because Smithy himself was a ghost, but whatever their motivation, the two friends felt it important that all ghosts be treated fairly.

Which, unfortunately, was why Denzel had ended up in here.

"Art thou going to say something?" asked the headless ghost on the other side of the table.

"Button it, punk!" spat Smithy. He was sitting beside Denzel, straddling a chair that he had turned the wrong way and chewing on a little wooden cocktail stick.

For some reason – Denzel wasn't sure why – Smithy was wearing sunglasses, and a little cardboard badge he'd made for himself that read "Bad Cop."

"I'm sorry?" asked the headless ghost. He was dressed

in Elizabethan-era finery, with a large white frilly collar around his neck stump.

"You heard me," Smithy growled. "Now, less of your lip or we'll throw the book at you."

Beneath the ghost's arm, his head frowned. "Which book?"

This caught Smithy off guard. He shot Denzel a sideways glance.

"I don't know yet," he admitted, then he narrowed his eyes and glared at the ghost. "But a big one. Like a cookbook. Yeah, a big hardback cookbook full of cake recipes. Would you like that, punk?"

"Not really," the ghost admitted.

Smithy slammed his hand on the table and jumped to his feet. "Answer the question!" he roared, his voice echoing around the room.

In the silence that followed, Denzel quietly cleared his throat. "Um, he did answer the question."

"Did he?" asked Smithy. "Oh. Sorry, wasn't listening. I was too busy thinking about cakes." He sat down and nodded politely to Denzel. "Continue."

Denzel smiled graciously, then flipped open a little notebook that sat on the table between him and the ghost.

"So, Mr... Um... Cassian De—"

"Do not speaketh my full name!" the ghost yelped.

Denzel jumped in fright at the sudden shout, then frowned. "Why not?"

The ghost shifted uncomfortably in his chair. "Because names have power, and I'd prefer you not to use mine." He smiled awkwardly. "Just 'Cassian' will be quite acceptable."

Denzel scribbled a little note next to the ghost's name, then continued.

"So, as you know, you were recently captured by the Spectre Collectors, having been caught in the act of..."

Denzel looked down at his notes. The words "Spectrothramorphic Transmogrification" were written there, but there was no chance of him getting through that without at least a week's rehearsal.

"...being a ghost," he finished.

"Guilty!" said Cassian's head.

"So you admit it?" Smithy barked. He cracked his knuckles. "Shame. I wanted to beat it out of you."

Denzel leaned back in his chair a little and whispered to Smithy. "We already knew he'd done it."

"Did we?" Smithy whispered back. "When?"

"Since Samara and Boyle caught him," Denzel continued.

"Oh. Right," said Smithy. He leaned in a little closer.

"Do you want me to beat him up anyway?"

Denzel shook his head. "No."

Smithy wiped a hand across his forehead. "Phew. That's a relief. He's terrifying."

He leaned in closer still. "I don't know if you've noticed, but he hasn't got a head! I mean, how does that work? How is he speaking? How does he hear what we're saying?"

Denzel flicked his gaze back to the ghost across the table. Cassian gave him a friendly little wave.

"His head's under his arm," Denzel pointed out.

"*Is it?*" said Smithy, much louder. He looked round at Cassian. "Ha! So it is! I didn't notice. It's right there!"

Denzel frowned. "How could you not have noticed?" he asked, then he sighed and shook his head. "Forget it. Doesn't matter. The point is, Cassian, you were doing ghost stuff, and it's our job to figure out if you're a good ghost or a bad ghost."

"Art thou serious?" asked Cassian. He glanced around at the drab little interview room he was being held in. Various enchantments and symbols had been scrawled on the walls to stop him escaping through one. "I was always under the impression that the Spectre Collectors were a 'catch first, asketh no questions ever' organisation. I assumed that my fate was already sealed."

"It would've been, until we came along," said Denzel. "We've convinced them that every ghost should be given a fair hearing."

"But I wish we hadn't!" Smithy spat, slamming his hand on the table again for good measure. "Scum like you, you make me *sick*."

Cassian's eyes slowly went from Smithy to Denzel. "Is he all right?"

Denzel smiled weakly. "Yeah. He wanted us to do Good Cop, Bad Cop. He's the Bad Cop."

"Don't tell him!" Smithy protested. "You'll ruin it."

"You're literally wearing a badge that says 'Bad Cop' on it," Denzel pointed out.

Smithy opened his mouth to offer a counterargument but came up short. Denzel had a point there.

"OK, yes, I'm Bad Cop," he admitted.

With a growl, Smithy reached across and took the notebook from the table. "Enough talk! Let's get down to business. We've prepared some questions to help us figure out your true motives. Answer them honestly, and we'll get along just fine. But lie to me, and I'll break you. *I will break you*. Understood?"

Cassian nodded to confirm that he understood.

Smithy cleared his throat and read from the top page. "OK. Question One. Are you a good ghost?"

"Yes," said Cassian.

Smithy scribbled with the pencil.

"Question Two. Are you a bad ghost?"

"No," said Cassian.

Smithy scribbled again.

"Right, then," he said. He smiled broadly, his aggressive Bad Cop persona vanishing. "Great! That's that settled."

Cassian's severed head blinked in surprise. "Is that it?"

"Yep," said Smithy. "All done!"

"Unless there's anything you want to add?" Denzel asked.

Cassian thought for a moment. "No. No, I think that's everything."

Smithy handed the notepad back to Denzel. As he took it, Denzel had a niggling suspicion that their questioning might not have been as probing as it possibly could have been, but this was their first ever interview, and they hadn't really known what to expect. They had another interview lined up in the cell next door. Maybe he'd come up with some more questions before then.

"Well, since you don't appear to be a threat to anyone, then you can leave," Denzel said.

"I can?" gasped the headless ghost. "Oh, that's wonderful news."

"I just need to read this," said Denzel, flipping to

the next page of the notepad. He blushed a little, embarrassed by the formality of it all. Still, rules were rules.

"By the power vested in me as a member of the Cult of Sh'grath, also known as the Messengers of the Allwhere, also known as the Seventh Army of the Enlightened—"

"And so on and so forth," added Smithy.

"And so on and so forth," Denzel agreed, skipping the rest of the paragraph. "I, Denzel Edgar, pronounce you, Cassian Deploop, a free ghost."

The final word had barely left Denzel's lips when Cassian exploded. At least, that was how it felt at the time.

In reality, he didn't explode. Technically, he turned inside out. Which, in many ways, was worse.

A bubbling green liquid erupted out through a hole in his neck, twisting and thrashing as it became a giant gooey blob. Teeth and eyes and snapping pincers all appeared in the slime. Three different mouths formed in the gelatinous folds, and all of them spoke at the same time.

"I warned you! I warned you not to say my name!" three distinct voices cried. "Now you leave me no choice but to destroy you!"

Neither Denzel nor Smithy had stood up yet. They

were both so transfixed by the horrifying transformation happening in front of them that it hadn't occurred to them to move.

That changed when the blobby Cassian-monster smashed a fist through the table, breaking it in two.

"Um, we should probably run," said Denzel.

"I like that plan," Smithy agreed.

Grabbing his friend by the hand, Smithy raced for the closest wall and threw them both towards it. Rather than slip through, they hit the wall with two short, solid *thunks*.

"Stupid enchantments," Smithy grumbled, rubbing his forehead.

He and Denzel both turned to find Cassian now almost completely filling one half of the room.

"Ugh, he's terrifying," said Smithy, pressing his back against the wall.

"Yep," Denzel agreed.

"It's like someone crossed a bogey with a load of lions," Smithy pointed out.

"Yep," Denzel agreed again.

"Here, what would you rather, right? Be eaten by a giant bogey crossed with a load of lions, or *eat* a giant bogey crossed with a load of—"

Cassian wasn't prepared to offer them the option.

His gooey green body grew a set of kangaroo-like legs and launched him across the room, all his many mouths opening wide to reveal all his many, *many* teeth.

Denzel and Smithy both raised their fists, closed their eyes and began punching frantically at thin air. They were both swinging wildly when they heard a short, sudden hiss, which was followed almost immediately by an angry shout and a heavy *thump*.

Opening one eye each, Denzel and Smithy saw the Cassian-creature being pinned down in the middle of the room by what looked like an explosion of shaving foam. He writhed on the floor, but no matter how hard he struggled, he couldn't pull himself free of the fizzing white foam.

The door to the interview room opened. Two Spectre Collectors entered – a boy in a blue and silver uniform, and a girl in a long, flowing red robe.

"Samara! Boyle!" Denzel gasped. "Thank God."

"Don't thank God, thank me," said Boyle, the boy in the uniform. He pointed to the ceiling, where a small nozzle dripped a final few blobs of the foam on to Cassian. "That was my idea."

"I made the foam," Samara pointed out. "So it was a joint effort."

"But I invented the delivery mechanism," said Boyle.

"So it was mostly me."

Sneering, he nudged Cassian with the toe of his boot. A string of sticky green gloop stuck to it.

"Oh, and in case you were wondering?" Boyle said to the helpless ghost. "Freedom revoked. You're totally going to the vault."

Cassian's many mouths sighed. "It's a fair cop, I suppose."

"There is no Fair Cop," Smithy growled. "Only Bad Cop and Good Cop."

He thought about this.

"Although, Good Cop is probably pretty fair, I suppose. Compared to Bad Cop, anyway."

He turned to the others to ask their opinion, and saw Boyle glaring at him.

"Don't you two have to be somewhere?" Boyle demanded.

Denzel took Smithy by the arm. "Uh, yes," he said, sliding along the wall towards the door and shrinking under Boyle's glare. "Come on, Smithy. That next ghost isn't going to interview itself!"

CHAPTER 2

Denzel and Smithy stood by the door of Interview Room Two, Denzel's hand resting on the handle.

"I don't think we should do Good Cop, Bad Cop any more," he said, not yet opening the door.

"I agree," said Smithy.

This caught Denzel off guard. "Really? I mean, you do? I mean, great."

"We should be Bad Cop and *Worse* Cop," Smithy suggested. "You be a bit mean and aggressive, and I'll set them on fire."

Denzel stared blankly back at him.

"Not *actual* fire, obviously," said Smithy.

"Oh. Good," said Denzel, relieved.

"Ghost fire."

"Right," said Denzel.

"Which is worse."

Part of Denzel was interested to know what made being set on ghost fire worse than being set on actual fire, but a much bigger part of him didn't want to find out.

"Let's just be ourselves," Denzel suggested. "And we'll see what happens."

Smithy sucked in his bottom lip as he thought about this. "OK, but you be me and I'll be you."

"Or I could be me, and you could be you," Denzel countered.

Smithy spat on his hand and held it out to Denzel. "Deal!"

They shook, then Denzel drew in a deep breath and opened the door to the interview room. Smithy went through first, and made it almost two whole steps before his entire world turned upside down and inside out, then spun in big looping circles around him.

"Uh..." he said. He said it for quite a long time, until he started to sound a bit like a broken robot.

His jaw had dropped open. His toes had curled up. His heart, which technically hadn't beaten in centuries, thumped against the inside of his chest.

There, sitting behind the table, was a girl.

No, not just *a* girl. That wasn't doing her justice. *The* girl, Smithy thought. The only girl in the whole wide world.

Sure, logically he knew that other girls probably existed, but right now he didn't ever remember seeing one before. At least, not one like this.

She sat bright and upright in her chair with her hands neatly crossed on the table in front of her. She was mostly solid, with just a hint of something glittery and sparkling playing across her smooth skin, and had a crop of red hair that made her look like her head was on fire. Ghost fire, if he was being specific.

Her nose swooped down and curved upwards at the end, like a perfect tiny ski slope. Above it, her eyes twinkled with mischief. Below it, her mouth was curled into a little smile that Smithy wanted to frame on his bedroom wall and look at forever.

"But not in a creepy way," he said aloud.

The girl and Denzel both looked confused.

"You what?" Denzel asked.

"Yes," said Smithy, still gazing in wonder at the ghost girl in the chair.

Denzel nudged him in the back, breaking the spell.

"Shift out of the way so I can get the door closed."

Smithy stared at his legs in surprise, like he'd only just remembered he had them. They plodded him over to one of the two empty chairs while Denzel closed the door. It locked with a *clunk*, securing the room.

Denzel smiled politely at the ghost girl and took his seat. Smithy was standing behind his own chair, leaning on the backrest as if he might fall over at any moment.

"Smithy?" Denzel said.

"Hmm?" said Smithy, still not taking his eyes off the girl. She regarded him curiously with one eyebrow raised.

"Is he OK?" the girl asked.

"HAHAHAHAHA! YES!" said Smithy, much too loudly.

Denzel sighed. "It's funny. I get asked that a lot."

"HAHAHAHAHA! YES!" said Smithy again.

He sat down suddenly, throwing himself on to the plastic seat like a finalist in the Musical Chairs World Cup.

Denzel watched him from the corner of his eye for a moment, then opened his notepad. "OK. Sorry about that," he began. "Tabitha?"

"Tabatha," the girl corrected.

Denzel frowned. "That's what I said."

"With an A," the girl explained.

Denzel's lips moved silently. "Tabitha always has an A. It's got two. Or have I been spelling it wrong?"

"HAHAHAHAHA! YES!" said Smithy, then he slapped himself across the face, looked momentarily surprised, and seemed to relax a little.

"T-A-B-A-T-H-A," Tabatha spelled out. "Three As."

"Ah. Right," said Denzel. He made a note in his pad, then smiled encouragingly. "So, you're probably wondering what's happening right now?"

Tabatha shrugged. "I was captured by the Spectre Collectors. Normally, I'd be flung straight into Spectral Storage, but..."

She looked Denzel and Smithy up and down. "You two came along and started something new."

She grinned broadly, showing off a mouth full of teeth that were just ever-so-slightly crooked, but which somehow made her even more perfect in Smithy's eyes.

"You know about the Spectre Collectors?" Denzel asked. "About us, I mean? You know who we are?"

Tabatha shrugged. "Let's just say this isn't my first run-in with you guys."

"Then how come you were roaming free?" Denzel wondered.

"Let's also say I'm good at escaping."

She leaned closer again. "Truth is, I've been keeping an eye on you. Your run-in with the director of this place, the thing with the shark and the Viking..."

"Wait," said Smithy. "What shark and Viking?"

Denzel eyed him for a moment, trying to work out if he was being serious. "In New York," he said. "The big ghost shark and ghost Viking we fought."

"Who, us?" asked Smithy.

"Yes," said Denzel.

Smithy continued to look blank.

"Have you been sniffing the memory dust?" Denzel asked. "We got recruited into the Spectre Collectors. We got sent to New York. A load of ghosts appeared, including a shark and a Viking. There was a big monkey."

"It's not ringing any bells," Smithy said.

Denzel sighed. "We had a pizza."

"Wait. Yes. Now I remember," said Smithy. He nodded encouragingly. "Continue."

"How do you know about all that stuff?" asked Denzel, turning back to Tabatha.

She shrugged and smiled at him. "I keep my ear to the ground," she said. "I know a lot of things."

Denzel got the impression she wasn't about to explain further, so he flipped open his notebook, ready to start writing.

"OK, so. Question One. Are you a good ghost, Tabatha?"

"Sometimes," Tabatha replied.

Denzel scribbled in the pad. "Are you a bad ghost?"

Tabatha's eyes twinkled. "Sometimes. Though never on Tuesdays."

Denzel stopped mid-scribble. "Why not Tuesdays?"

"On Tuesdays, I save the world," Tabatha said, quite matter-of-factly.

Smithy stared in wonder. "What, every Tuesday?"

"Most Tuesdays," Tabatha said. "And not always this world."

"What do you save it from?" Smithy wondered.

Tabatha made a little weighing motion with her hands. "Depends on the Tuesday."

Denzel had a horrible feeling this interview was already starting to get away from him. He looked down at his notes until he found what Tabatha was being charged with. Unfortunately, he couldn't even begin to think about how to pronounce it. It started with *ecto* and ended with *diaphantomism*, but everything in between may as well have been a string of gibberish.

The good ghost/bad ghost questions hadn't really helped figure out Tabatha's motives. He had no choice. He'd have to dig deeper, and that meant going off-script.

"So," Denzel said, his mind racing as he tried to come up with some more questions. "Ghosts."

Tabatha and Smithy both looked at him. From their expressions, they were clearly expecting some sort of follow-up, but Denzel had already drawn a blank. He raised his eyebrows and stared expectantly at them.

"What about them?" asked Tabatha.

"Um, what do you think of them?" Denzel asked.

Tabatha's eyes met Smithy's. It was, Smithy thought, the greatest moment of his afterlife.

"Some of them are all right," she said. "Some of them aren't."

"Why are you still asking her questions?" Smithy wondered. "You heard her, she saves the world every Tuesday! She's obviously good."

Denzel leaned in closer to his friend and lowered his voice to a whisper. "Yes, but she doesn't really, does she? She's just saying that."

Something solid *clonked* Denzel on the head. He looked across the table to find Tabatha wielding a little walking cane with a shiny gold fist on the end. He rubbed his head where the knuckles had rapped him.

"It's rude to whisper," Tabatha said.

"Where did you get that from?" Denzel demanded.

Tabatha folded the cane in half, then squashed both ends together between her palms, vanishing it like a magician's wand.

"Where did I get what?" she asked innocently. She leaned back in her chair. "And no, I'm not 'just saying that'. I save the world every Tuesday. Fact."

"How? From what? And why only Tuesdays?" Denzel demanded, still rubbing his head.

Tabatha counted on her fingers. "That varies. That also varies. And because Tuesdays are dangerous, obviously." She snorted. "Everyone knows that."

Denzel's face made it very clear that he still wasn't buying it. Tabatha sighed.

"OK, take last Tuesday," she said, jabbing a thumb back over her shoulder as if that particular day was right behind her somewhere. "Remember when those Void Hippos trampled all over the timestream?"

Denzel and Smithy exchanged glances.

"No," said Denzel.

Tabatha flashed them a beaming smile. "I rest my case," she said, and something inside Smithy melted when she winked at him.

"She saved the timestream, Denzel!" Smithy yelped. "From Void Hippos!"

"What are Void Hippos?" Denzel asked.

"Does it matter? She stopped them!" Smithy continued. "We have to let her go!"

Denzel was less sure. "Let's not rush into it," he

suggested. "We don't know enough about her yet."

From outside in the corridor, there came a *thump* and a roar.

"What's that?" Tabatha asked.

"The guy next door," Denzel explained. "We said his name and it turned him into a big monster."

Tabatha nodded sagely. "Ah. Yeah, that can happen. They're powerful things, names."

The door to the interview room shook. A raised voice – Boyle's, Denzel thought – shouted, "Stand down!" in quite an angry way.

Denzel and Smithy's chairs creaked as they turned to look in the direction of the sound. That was why they were looking straight at the door when it exploded off its hinges and a blubbery lump of green goo forced its way inside, shrugging off a couple of Spectre Collectors who had jumped on to its back.

Its countless teeth bared when it saw Denzel. Four Hulk-like arms sprouted from its blobby body, the thick fingers balling into fists as the monster hurled itself at the boys.

"He is coming!" hissed a multitude of voices from the thing's many mouths. "He is coming!"

Denzel tried to jump clear, but the Cassian-blob was too close, moving too fast. He cried out in panic as a slimy hand clamped down on the top of his head, and then all he could see were teeth as the monster lunged.

KER-SPLAT!

The creature exploded, and several hundred litres of green gunge splattered across Denzel, Smithy and the rest of the room. In that order.

For a moment, Denzel just stood there, frozen to the spot, his breath coming in deep, panicky gulps.

At last, he turned slowly to find Tabatha on her feet, her cane held in one hand. The forefinger of the little golden fist was extended. Denzel and Smithy both watched a curl of smoke rise from it, before the finger tucked back into the fist and a thumb raised instead.

"You're welcome," said Tabatha. She folded the cane up until it vanished, then sat down and nodded in the direction of Denzel's slime-coated notepad. "Saved your life," she said, her big, broad, beamer of a smile returning. "You might want to write that down."

CHAPTER 3

"I don't like it," said Boyle. He, Samara and Denzel were in one of the underground complex's security rooms, watching the camera feed from the interview room where Tabatha was being held. Smithy had stayed behind to "keep an eye on her". He seemed to be taking this literally, as he'd done nothing but stare at her for the past six minutes, and showed no signs of stopping.

"To be fair, you don't like anything," Samara said. "And she did save Denzel."

"I had it under control," Boyle insisted.

"It didn't feel very under control when that thing had my whole head in its hand," Denzel pointed out.

"We would have stopped it," said Boyle.

"What, before it had cracked Denzel's skull open like an egg, or after?" asked Samara. She turned to Denzel, ignoring Boyle's continued protests. "What did you say her name was?"

"Tabatha," said Denzel. "With an A."

"Tabitha always has an A," said Boyle.

"T-A-B-A-T-H-A," Denzel recited.

For some reason, this just seemed to annoy Boyle more. He tutted and shook his head, but said nothing.

"She said she saved the timestream from Void Hippos last Tuesday," said Denzel.

He had been expecting them to laugh at that, so the serious glance they shared surprised him. "What?" he asked. "She didn't, did she?"

"Hard to say," said Samara. "Dangerous things."

"Void Hippos?" said Denzel.

"Tuesdays," Samara corrected. "But yes, also Void Hippos."

Denzel's jaw dropped. "You're not seriously telling me that Void Hippos exist?"

"Of course they don't exist," Boyle snapped. "She's delusional."

Denzel pointed to Samara. "What, her?"

"No, her," said Boyle, gesturing to the screen, where

Smithy was still staring wistfully at Tabatha.

Samara smirked. "Yeah, sorry. I was winding you up. Never heard of Void Hippos."

She clicked her tongue against the back of her teeth a few times, then nodded. "We should keep her around though. Study her a bit more."

"What?!" Boyle spluttered. "You want us to keep *another* ghost around the place? Spectre Collectors doesn't mean we collect them for fun! They're not stamps! We're supposed to lock them up."

Samara and Denzel both frowned.

"You collect stamps?" asked Samara.

"For *fun*?" Denzel added.

"Shut up," Boyle grunted.

"You do know what fun is, yes?" Denzel asked him. "You do understand the concept?"

Boyle crossed his arms over his Vulteron uniform. "I don't trust her. And I don't think we should be keeping more ghosts around the place. Especially crazy ones."

"She might be crazy, but she's powerful," Samara said.

Boyle narrowed his eyes. "All the more reason to lock her in Spectral Storage. We can't just leave her to wander around the place."

Samara tucked her thumbs into the rope-belt that was tied around her tunic. Lots of little bags containing magical powders and potions hung from it.

"The Elders put Denzel in charge of deciding ghosts' fates. It's up to him." She raised her eyebrows. "Denzel? What do you say?"

Denzel groaned inwardly. It was absolutely right, he thought, that ghosts should be given a fair chance. For centuries, the Spectre Collectors had just assumed they were all bad and locked them away, but Smithy had proved that being a ghost didn't automatically make you evil.

Yes, a lot of the time it did, but not always, and that was the point.

While Denzel thought all ghosts should be given a fair hearing, he didn't like being the one doing the listening. Deciding their fates was a big responsibility, and while some of them – Stabby, the octopus-ghost with knives for arms he'd met yesterday, for example – obviously had to be locked away for everyone's safety, some cases were less clear-cut.

He'd almost set Cassian free, and look how he'd turned out. Sure, Tabatha seemed nice enough right now, but what if she turned into some crazy green blob like he had? Wouldn't it just be safer to let Boyle sling her in Spectral Storage?

On the screen, Smithy sighed dreamily. Tabatha

smiled awkwardly at him, then shot a sideways look to the camera and quietly mouthed, "Help."

Denzel groaned again – outwardly, this time.

"Fine. Let's not lock her up quite yet."

"Good," said Samara. She stuck her tongue out at Boyle, then gave Denzel a playful punch on the arm. "You and Smithy can look after her."

With that, Samara turned and strode off along the corridor.

"Wait, what?" Denzel called after her, but before he could hear if she answered, Boyle prodded him in the chest.

"You'd better not mess this up, Denzel," he warned. "Anything that spook does is now your responsibility. She goes on a murderous rampage? Your fault. She cracks open Spectral Storage and floods the place with ghosts? That's on you."

Denzel swallowed, his mouth suddenly dry. "Please don't say that."

"Here, hold this," said Boyle, thrusting a closed fist in Denzel's direction, thumb down.

Denzel eyed the hand warily. "What is it?"

"Just take it," Boyle growled.

Cautiously, Denzel cupped his hands under Boyle's fist. The bigger boy opened the fist to reveal nothing at all.

"That's the fate of the world," Boyle told him. "It's now in your hands."

Denzel gazed down at his empty cupped palms. "I don't want it in my hands."

Boyle backed away after Samara, raising his arms as if in a gesture of surrender. "It's in your hands, Denzel. It's too late. It's in your hands."

Denzel remained frozen to the spot, his hands still cupped in front of him, his eyes wide in panic. "Can you take it back?"

"No. Now, get Smithy and his girlfriend, and bring them to the briefing room," Boyle ordered.

"What? Why?"

"Because that 'He is coming' thing people keep saying to you?" said Boyle. "We think we've figured it out."

CHAPTER 4

Denzel had stood rooted to the spot for a full two minutes, wondering where he should put the fate of the world, before realising that Boyle had been speaking metaphorically, and that he wasn't actually holding anything at all. In hindsight, that should've been obvious, but when you were surrounded by invisible ghosts, magic and insanely advanced technology all day, it was sometimes difficult to know what was real and what wasn't.

In the end, and just to be on the safe side, he'd put the fate of the world in his pocket. Then he'd rounded up Smithy, given Tabatha the good news that she wasn't going to spend eternity in ghost prison, and invited them both to join him in the briefing room.

Unfortunately, the Spectre Collector's HQ was a vast underground complex, and it turned out that there was more than one briefing room. There were more than ten briefing rooms, in fact, and it had taken almost half an hour for them to find the one Boyle had been referring to.

When they eventually stumbled in, the expression on Boyle's face revealed just how furious he was at the delay. Denzel wanted to point out that it was entirely Boyle's own fault for not being more specific, but thought it safest not to.

To Denzel's disappointment, Boyle wasn't actually the meanest person in the room. Two other Spectre Collectors sat at chairs around a polished wooden table. They both sneered at Denzel when he walked in, then jumped to their feet at the sight of Tabatha.

"Unauthorised Vaporous Entity!" barked Knightley. She was a Vulteron, like Boyle, and took aim at Tabatha with a blaster pistol.

Beside Knightley, her Oberon partner, Rasmus, waved his arms threateningly, light sparkling around his fingertips. "I sense Class Five Spectral Energy levels," he warned.

"Is Class Five a good level of Spectral Energy?" Tabatha asked no one in particular. "How does the rating work?"

Smithy shrugged. "Nobody knows."

"Yes, we do know, and yes, it is," said Samara. She gestured for Knightley and Rasmus to sit down. "She's fine. She's been authorised."

"By *who*?" Knightley demanded.

Boyle pointed to Denzel. "By him."

Knightley and Rasmus both turned slowly in Denzel's direction. If looks could kill – and in Rasmus's case, they might – Denzel would've been dead on the spot.

"You let a Level Five Spectral Entity roam free?" Knightley spat.

"Inside our headquarters?" added Rasmus, his wispy teenage moustache bristling with disgust.

Denzel shifted uncomfortably. "She's, uh, she's fine. She's nice," he said.

"Lovely," Smithy added with a sigh. He smiled longingly up at the much taller Tabatha. She gave him a double thumbs-up in response.

"Thanks for the support," she said, then she waved to the others. "Nice to meet you. Tabatha Tarrin. Ghost."

"She saves the world on Tuesdays," Smithy added.

"*Most* Tuesdays," Tabatha clarified.

"From Void Hippos," said Smithy.

"Sometimes from Void Hippos. Not exclusively," said Tabatha.

Knightley and Rasmus shot each other sideways looks. They both nodded.

"Not buying it. I'm taking her out!" Knightley barked.

Her finger squeezed the trigger of her weapon and Denzel felt like the world went into slow motion.

A bolt of blue light spat from the end and went streaking in Tabatha's direction.

Smithy jumped, throwing himself in front of the ghost girl with a long, drawn-out, "Nooooooo!"

Luckily for him, he completely misjudged the timing and landed heavily on the floor, the bolt whistling past above him, still on target.

Denzel let out a little gasp of wonder as Tabatha spun, producing her cane from nowhere. She swung it with one hand, deflecting the blaster bolt up towards the ceiling.

All eyes followed it as it went up, up, up, then the bolt hit the light fitting and with a *BANG* the room was plunged into darkness.

The emergency lights kicked in less than a second later. By the time they had, Tabatha stood behind Knightley, her cane raised. The hand on the end was making a gun-shape with its forefinger and thumb, and this was now jammed up against the back of Knightley's head.

Rasmus began to turn, his fingers glowing with magical energy.

"I wouldn't," Tabatha warned. She was smiling, and looked really quite relaxed about the whole situation.

Rasmus froze for a moment, then let his hands fall to his sides.

"Much appreciated," Tabatha told him. She flicked her eyes to Knightley, her smile still fixed in place. "What I don't appreciate, though, is being shot at for no reason."

"You're a *ghost*," hissed Knightley through clenched teeth.

"Now, that's just deadist," Tabatha told her. "Just because I'm deceased, it doesn't make me a bad person. What is this, the eighteen fifties?"

She removed the cane from the back of Knightley's skull. The hand became a fist again.

"Now, I'm going to go ahead and assume this was all just a misunderstanding that we're going to put behind us, and that from now on we're going to be the best of friends. OK?"

Knightley spun and brought up her blaster. Or, at least, she tried to.

"Looking for this?" asked Tabatha, holding up the weapon. She twirled it around her finger a few times like a cowboy, then presented it back to Knightley, handle first. Tabatha smiled, showing off her uneven teeth. "Like I said, just a misunderstanding."

She tapped the cane gently on top of Knightley's head, said, "Boop!" in a high-pitched voice, then took a seat in one of the chairs arranged around the table. Knightley stared at her gun in disbelief, saying nothing.

"Now then," Tabatha began, resting her elbows on the table and steepling her fingers in front of her. "What's all this about?"

Smithy was floating several centimetres above the ground, his eyes practically transforming into little love hearts. With a sigh, Denzel caught him by the sleeve and gently tugged him down to Earth again.

"It's funny you should ask," Denzel said. "I was wondering the same thing."

Boyle gestured for everyone to sit. Smithy hurried to sit in the chair closest to Tabatha, and Denzel sat in the next one along. Knightley and Rasmus both looked awkward for a few moments, then sat back down in their own seats again.

With a gesture, Boyle indicated a screen mounted on the wall. A series of cryptic symbols were displayed on it. They seemed to have been carved into a chunk of stone, and Denzel had no idea what any of them meant.

"Any idea what that is?" Boyle asked.

Smithy's hand shot up. "A big telly," he said.

Boyle held his gaze for quite a long time. "No," he eventually said with a heavy sigh. "It's not a big telly."

"It is," Smithy insisted. "It must be at least fifty inches."

The remote control, which Boyle was holding, went *crack* in his grip.

"I think what Boyle's asking," said Samara, jumping in before her partner could start shouting. "Is if you know what's *on* the big telly?"

Smith's hand went up again. "Dust?" he guessed.

"No..." said Samara, as patiently as possible

"Is it writing?" asked Denzel, before Smithy could say more.

"Obviously, it's writing," said Rasmus. He leaned closer and lowered his head a fraction, as if peering at the screen over the top of a pair of glasses. "Ancient Sumarian, unless I'm very much mistaken. Which I rarely am."

Samara tried not to show her annoyance. "Right. It's Ancient Sumarian. Dates from around eight thousand BC. But that's not the interesting thing."

Denzel was relieved that this wasn't the interesting thing, mostly because as things went it wasn't very interesting. The writing just looked like a few squiggly lines, as far as he was concerned, and he didn't see what it had to do with ... well, anything at all.

"It was found in Scotland," said Samara.

Across the table, Rasmus, Knightley and Tabatha all reacted in surprise. Smithy, who didn't want to be left out, gasped loudly.

"Scotland!" he said. He shook his head and puffed out his cheeks in amazement. "Scotland, Scotland, Scotland."

Everyone sat staring at him as he adopted a terrible Scottish accent and began reciting words at random. "Och! Hoots! Haggis! Um... Kilts!"

He ran out of Scottish things to say then. "That's me done," he said. "Continue."

Samara began to speak. "So—"

"Bagpipes!" Smithy announced.

Samara watched him to make sure he was really finished this time, then continued.

"So I know what you're all wondering," she said.

"When's lunch?" Denzel quipped, then he wilted under the weight of the Spectre Collectors' stares. "Kidding!" he added weakly.

Samara rolled her eyes. "You're wondering how Ancient Sumerian text from eight thousand years before the birth of Christ ended up in Scotland."

"That's definitely the other thing I was wondering,"

Denzel said, even though it definitely wasn't. "How did that happen?"

"We don't know," Boyle said. "It doesn't make sense. And yet, it's there."

Knightley, who had still seemed to be in a state of shock ever since the "boop" incident, shot Boyle a narrow-eyed glare. "Where is it?"

Smithy's hand went up. "On the telly," he said. He pointed. "See?"

Knightley didn't bother trying to hide her contempt. "I meant, where was the image captured? Where is the writing?"

Smithy raised a hand again. Knightley cut him off before he could speak. "If you're going to say Scotland, I *will* shoot you. One and only warning."

Smithy lowered his hand and smiled sheepishly at Tabatha. "She's actually very fond of me."

"I'm not," Knightley said.

"She is," Smithy insisted. He lowered his voice to a whisper and leaned in close to the ghost girl. "But it's a secret."

Tabatha regarded him in silence for a few moments. "You are a strange little person," she told him, then that big smile of hers lit up the room. "I like you."

Smithy's head flopped down and hit the table with a

thunk. He lay there, unmoving, a goofy grin plastered across his face.

"Aaaanyway," said Samara, continuing. "The text was found in a cave in the Highlands. Now, the *where* may be interesting, but it's the *what* that'll blow your mind."

She gestured to the screen. "It took a while, but we translated it. Boyle."

Boyle tapped a couple of buttons on his remote control and the still image became moving footage. As they all watched, the squiggles squirmed around, all but one turning into neatly carved letters.

Denzel's chair creaked as he leaned forward. His heart somehow managed to leap into his throat and sink down into his stomach at the same time.

The words on screen were ones he knew well. Lately, it seemed that he was hearing them everywhere he went. And now, there they were, carved in an ancient dead language on a wall somewhere in Scotland. It was a message, and he somehow knew that despite being eight thousand years old, the message was meant for him.

Denzel's voice came as a shaky croak as he read the words aloud.

"He is coming."

A silence fell across the room. It was eventually broken

38

by Smithy suddenly sitting upright and saying, "She likes me," as a long, happy sigh.

"What does that last one mean?" Denzel asked, pointing to the only symbol that hadn't been translated. As he squinted, it sort of looked like an upside-down skull. Something about it made something unpleasant stir deep down in his stomach.

"We don't know," Samara admitted. "It's cropped up in Sumerian text for thousands of years, but we've never been able to translate it."

Beside him, Tabatha leaned forward in her chair, her brow furrowed as she stared at the symbol.

"Do you know what it means?" Denzel asked her.

Tabatha blinked in surprise. "Hmm? Oh, no," she said, leaning back. "Never seen it before in my afterlife."

Denzel nodded slowly. Hopefully the symbol meant something nice, but he seriously doubted it. He looked from Samara to Boyle and back again.

"So what happens now?" he asked.

"Marriage, probably," said Smithy. He smiled at Tabatha, whose eyes were wide with worry.

"I meant about 'He is coming'," Denzel said, looking at the others. "What happens now?"

Boyle straightened, standing to attention. "Now, we go to Scotland."

CHAPTER
5

Denzel had never been to Scotland before. Not that
he could remember, anyway. In fact, he'd never even
really thought about the place much, other than to
maintain a sort of low-level knowledge that it existed.
He remembered his dads explaining that it was so far
north you had to drive past all the motorway signs that
said "The North" and then just keep going.

It was so far north, they said, that "The North" was
south. Denzel hadn't really understood that at the time.
And, now that he was actually standing in Scotland, he
still didn't. This was mostly because they hadn't spent
several hours driving, and had instead spent one minute

and eleven seconds travelling through some sort of magic tunnel that Samara had magicked up.

Afterwards, Denzel had described the trip as "an interesting experience". By which he meant he had spent the first forty seconds crying, and then vomited twice. He was hopeful that on the way home he could convince everyone to let him take the bus.

They stood on a hill now – Denzel, Smithy, Samara, Boyle and Tabatha – gazing down at a lush green glen below. It stretched out for what seemed like fifty miles of trees and rivers and fields, before meeting a range of mountains rising up at the other side.

"Pretty amazing, isn't it?" said Samara.

Boyle gave a disinterested grunt and busied himself with a handheld scanning device. He'd been pushing buttons and tapping the screen for a good hour now, but if it had told him anything, he wasn't sharing it.

Smithy and Denzel had clambered up on to a boulder to get a better look at the scenery below. As they stood taking it all in, Smithy gave Denzel a nudge. "Here, Denzel, look."

He pointed off into the middle distance.

"Sheep."

Denzel followed his finger, then nodded. "Yep. That's a sheep, all right."

Smithy nudged him again. "Look! Look!" His finger moved a tiny distance to the right. "Another sheep."

Denzel smiled as patiently as possible. "Sure is."

"Oh! Oh! Denzel!" said Smithy, nudging him yet again. "Another sheep."

"That's a big rock," said Denzel.

Smithy's eyes widened, a big rock apparently even more exciting to him than a boring old sheep.

"No *way*!" he gasped. Wheeling around, he addressed the others. "Guys! You're not going to believe this! There's a big rock!"

Samara and Boyle, who now knew Smithy well enough to completely ignore most of what he said, completely ignored what he'd said.

Tabatha, to Smithy's delight, took an interest and followed his trembling finger all the way to the curved white stone. "Meh. I've seen bigger," she said.

Smithy's jaw dropped. "That's impossible!"

"What are you talking about?" Denzel asked. "It's not even that big. It's just a rock."

"That's the biggest rock anyone's ever seen," Smithy insisted. "Fact."

"What about that one?" asked Tabatha. She pointed to the boulder that Smithy and Denzel were standing on. It was the size of a small elephant.

"Oh," said Smithy, after a while. "Right."

He turned to face front again. "Still. Nice, isn't it? Scotland?"

Denzel nodded. It *was* nice. It was beautiful.

"Bit wet though," he remarked.

"Oh God, yeah," said Smithy. "Bit wet."

They both looked up into the relentless drizzle that had been soaking them to the skin for the past twenty minutes. They had barely been in Scotland for an hour, and had already encountered four different types of rain, each one worse than the one before.

To start with, Samara had conjured up a shimmering magical shield that hung above them like an umbrella, but then a big gust of wind had come along and blown it away, and Boyle had been forced to chase it down and shoot it before anyone saw it.

Not that there was anyone around to see much of anything. Denzel had an uninterrupted view for miles in every direction, and there wasn't a road or building to be seen, much less any people.

If he'd been asked to describe Scotland in three words, Denzel would've said, "Beautiful, empty and wet." If he'd been asked to describe it in five words, he'd have said "wet" again twice.

Seriously, did it *ever* stop raining?

Denzel was about to ask Samara if she could conjure up some sunshine when Boyle's device gave out a series of urgent-sounding *bleeps*.

"What *is* that thing?" asked Tabatha, standing on her tiptoes to get a better look at the gadget. Boyle glowered at her, then turned away, shielding it with his body so she couldn't see it.

"I'm getting Spectral Energy readings," said Boyle. "Faint, but they're there."

Smithy and Tabatha both raised their hands.

"No, it's not you two," Boyle spat. "I'm not an idiot." He shot Samara a sideways glance. "Why have we even brought her along, anyway? We don't know anything about her."

Samara shrugged. "Like you said, she's too dangerous to leave wandering around the place. This way, we can keep an eye on her."

Above them, the relentless drizzle became a punishing downpour. Denzel pulled his jacket up over his head and shot Boyle a pleading look.

"So, this Spectral Energy you found," he said, shouting to make himself heard above the roaring of the rain. "I don't suppose it's somewhere warm and dry?"

"Somehow, this is actually worse," Denzel whispered.

His voice hissed back to him off the uneven stone walls of a narrow tunnel that led from a cave down into the hillside.

The rain couldn't reach down here, but a cold wind whistled after them, as if urging them to go deeper. Denzel picked his way carefully through the gloom, tripping every few steps on some rocky outcrop, or sliding on loose gravel. Smithy clung closely to him, while Tabatha walked ahead, as sure-footed as a goat.

Boyle took the lead up front, two torches on his shoulders cutting cones of light through the darkness. Samara followed behind Denzel and Smithy, her fingers dancing as she conjured a shimmering blue glow that painted the walls around them.

"Anything?" Samara called to the front.

Boyle consulted his gizmo. "Trace readings. Not a lot."

Tabatha skipped between a couple of rocks and looked around at the narrow walls. "This place seems familiar," she said.

Smithy tensed. "It's not going to be full of Void Hippos, is it?"

Tabatha shook her head. "No, it's... I dunno. It just reminds me of something."

"A scary cave?" Denzel guessed.

"Dying," said Smithy, after a moment.

Tabatha slowed to look back at him. "Huh?"

"It reminds me of dying," Smithy said. "When I died, there was a tunnel I think I was supposed to follow." He wrinkled his nose. "I didn't much like the look of it, so I went somewhere else."

"You went somewhere else?" said Denzel. "Where?"

Smithy tried to remember. "Blackpool, I think."

"You died and went to *Blackpool*?"

Smithy nodded. "They've got donkeys," he said, as if this was the only explanation anyone would need.

"You're right," said Tabatha.

"I know I am. You can ride them along the beach," Smithy replied.

Tabatha shook her head. "No, not about the donkeys. I mean about the dying thing. That's what it reminds me of." She took another look around them. "The tunnel. You're right."

They walked on, Boyle checking his gadgets as he led the way.

"How did you two end up with these guys?" Tabatha asked, gesturing to the Spectre Collectors.

"I thought you knew?" said Denzel.

"Some of it. Not all," Tabatha replied. "Humour me."

"I saw a ghost," Denzel explained. "In my living room. They turned up and caught it."

SPECTRE COLLECTORS

"And then a load of rubbish came out of a bin and tried to grab him," Smithy added.

"So they recruited us," said Denzel. "Well, mostly me."

"And he wanted to leave, so their boss did something to Denzel's parents to make them forget he'd ever existed. Right, Denzel?"

Denzel's jaw tightened. His voice, when it came, was a thin croak. "Yeah. Yeah, that's right."

"You people made his parents forget him?" Tabatha gasped. "That's pretty horrible."

"It wasn't *us*," Samara protested. "We wouldn't do that. We tried to help fix it but, well..."

"They couldn't," said Denzel.

"No," said Samara, smiling sadly back at him. "We couldn't."

Denzel shrugged. "And so here we are."

"That's quite a story," said Tabatha. "Sorry for your loss."

They plodded on in silence for a while, Boyle leading them downward into the dark.

"Speaking of loss, how did you die?" asked Denzel. "If you don't mind me asking?"

Tabatha raised her head proudly. "Stopping a bank robbery."

"Whoa! Seriously?" Smithy gasped.

"Yeah. Actually, it was a double bank robbery. I won't bore you with the details," Tabatha said. "Pretty heroic, though, if I do say so myself. What about you, Smithy? How did you bite the big one?"

"Diarrhoea, mostly," said Smithy.

"Oh," said Tabatha.

"And then I coughed myself inside out."

"Right," said Tabatha. "That's … impressive."

Smithy bowed. "I thank you."

"Everyone shut up," Boyle commanded.

Denzel dropped his voice to a whisper. "Have you found something?" he asked, peering into the darkness beyond where Boyle's torchlight ended.

"No," Boyle replied. "I just don't want to listen to you any more. You're all annoying me."

He stopped abruptly. "Wait. Hold up."

The device in his hand *buzzed* urgently.

"What does that noise mean?" Smithy asked. "Is that a good noise? It doesn't sound like a good noise."

"Spectral Energy spike," said Boyle.

At the rear of the line, the fine hairs on the back of Samara's neck stood on end. "I'm getting it too," she said. "I think there's something down here with—"

Before she could finish, a blurry white shape emerged from the wall, slammed into her and whisked her straight

48

through the opposite wall.

"Everyone down!" Boyle barked, spinning and raising his rifle. The gadget he was carrying *screeched* out an alarm as another white shape exploded up from the floor beneath him.

Boyle opened fire, sending a volley of glowing red energy bolts screaming along the passageway, forcing Denzel, Smithy and Tabatha to duck for cover.

When the gunfire stopped, they all cautiously raised their heads. Boyle, like Samara, was gone. The spot where he had been standing was empty, aside from a single torch that spun on the floor, sending shadows scurrying across the walls.

"Uh, guys," Smithy whispered, his voice sounding unnaturally loud in the narrow tunnel. "I don't want to alarm anyone, but I *think* we might be in trouble."

CHAPTER 6

A few moments after Samara and Boyle had been taken, the whispers started.

"He is coming."

"He is coming."

"He is coming."

Denzel and Smithy drew closer together, grabbing at each other in panic. Their eyes darted this way and that, trying to figure out which direction the sounds were coming from. The way the whispering bounced around inside the confined space made it impossible to pinpoint.

There was a faint *whum* as Tabatha produced her cane and spun it around her finger a couple of times.

She stood rigid and upright in the middle of the tunnel, her eyes closed, her head cocked so that one ear was pointing upwards.

"This way," she said, doing a crisp about-turn and creeping ahead along the tunnel. As she passed the torch, she flicked it backwards with her cane, and Denzel scrambled to catch it.

"Wait, what?" he whispered, shining the torch after her. "That's not the way out. Shouldn't we be looking for the way out?"

"You're not going to find your friends outside," Tabatha told him. She made a clicking noise with her mouth, like someone calling to a pony. "This way. Come on. Giddy-up."

Smithy turned to Denzel, his face a picture of excitement. "She made a horsey noise!" he said, then he turned and cantered after her before Denzel could reply.

"So?! That doesn't mean we should follow her!" Denzel whimpered, but Smithy continued to trot after Tabatha, leaving him behind.

Denzel swept the torch across the spots where Samara and Boyle had vanished. He looked both ways along the tunnel. Then, with a groan, he hurried after his two ghost companions, the torchlight trembling across the walls ahead of him.

"He is coming."

"He is coming."

"He is coming."

As Denzel closed the gap, the whispering seemed to come from all around them – ahead, behind and seeping through the very rock itself.

They crept along the passageway, Denzel and Smithy close together, Tabatha leading the way. Soon the tunnel walls grew narrower, forcing Denzel to hold his breath and try to squeeze himself through a tight space between two bulges in the walls.

He pushed, he heaved, he struggled and then, all of a sudden, he found himself stuck.

"Hey, wait for me!" he whispered, squirming and wriggling as he tried to force his way through the narrow gap. Gritting his teeth, he kicked harder with his feet, trying to force his way through using sheer brute strength.

Unfortunately, brute strength was never really his strong point. Rather than push his way through to the other side of the narrowing spot, he wedged himself more tightly into it. His chest and back were so tightly pinned that he couldn't breathe. His face was all squashed up, and one arm was pinned awkwardly behind him.

Well, wasn't this just great?

"Help!" he managed to wheeze.

The others stopped and doubled back. "What's the matter?" Smithy asked.

Denzel couldn't move his head, but managed to look down at himself using just his eyes.

"Thtuck," he said, through his squished-up mouth.

Smithy frowned. "What?"

"I'm thtuck."

Smithy's eyes narrowed in concentration. "Something about a duck?"

'Not thtuck. *Thtuck.*'

"I can't hear you properly. Your face is all squashed between those big rocks," Smithy told him.

Tabatha stepped past Smithy and placed a hand on Denzel's head. Denzel became intangible like a ghost and instantly fell through the rocks. By the time he clattered on to the ground, he was solid again.

"Oh, you were *stuck*!" Smithy realised. "You should've just said."

Tabatha placed a finger to her lips and tightened her grip on her cane. There was a bend in the tunnel up ahead, and she motioned for Denzel and Smithy to follow as she sneaked towards it.

While he was stuck in the rocks, all Denzel had been able to hear was the thumping of his own heartbeat in his ears, and a worrying *creaking* noise that his skull had been making.

Now he was out, he could hear something else too. Voices. Not whispering this time, but … singing?

No, not singing either, he realised. They were chanting.

"Stay quiet, stay low," Tabatha instructed.

Denzel ducked into a crouch. Smithy sank into the floor all the way up to his knees.

"Handy, this ghost thing," he whispered back to Denzel.

He turned to find Tabatha glaring at him. "Stay *quieter*," she urged.

Smithy mimed zipping his mouth shut.

Then he mimed fastening a tiny padlock to it.

Then he mimed locking the padlock and throwing away the key.

"Done," he said, instantly making the entire mime a complete waste of time.

Tabatha's glare became a raised eyebrow and a half-smile, then she became serious again and gestured to the bend ahead. "Stick close. Don't make any sudden movements. We don't want them to know we're here."

"They already know we're here!" Denzel squeaked. "They took Samara and Boyle."

Tabatha shook her head and pointed back up

the tunnel. "They know we were *there*. They don't necessarily know we're *here*. Now, come on."

She raised her cane and the hand on the end made a beckoning motion with one finger, signalling for Denzel and Smithy to follow.

They crept together through the tunnel. Denzel kept his torch pointed to the floor so that he could see some of what was ahead of him without shining a beam of light directly ahead that might give them away.

The closer they got to the bend, the louder the chanting became. It was in some sort of foreign language that Denzel didn't recognise. If he'd had to guess, he'd have said Ancient Sumerian, but for all he knew it might equally have been Welsh.

Tabatha reached the bend in the tunnel and stopped. The hand on her cane opened up fully, gesturing for Denzel and Smithy to halt.

After placing her finger to her lips again and glaring pointedly at Smithy, Tabatha sank backwards into the wall and vanished. The torchlight trembled on the floor as Denzel and Smithy waited.

And waited.

And waited.

"She's not coming back," Denzel whispered.

"Of course she is," said Smithy. "She wouldn't leave

me. We're practically married."

"You aren't," Denzel told him.

"We *practically* are," Smithy insisted.

Both boys jumped in fright when Tabatha stepped through the wall again, her eyes alive with excitement.

"You have *got* to see this," she told them, grabbing them both by the wrists. Denzel barely had time to take a big breath before he was yanked into the rock.

For a few seconds, he saw nothing but blurry darkness, and then he emerged into a wider opening in the tunnel. Light danced and flickered across the walls and ceiling. It came from a much larger cave chamber, which Denzel only got a brief glimpse of before Tabatha pulled him and Smithy to the floor.

The tunnel opened high up in the cave wall, so that when Denzel, Smithy and Tabatha crawled to the ledge, they had a bird's-eye view of what was going on below.

Quite what *was* going on below, Denzel didn't know. But he felt it was safe to say that it was nothing good.

Samara and Boyle were tied, back-to-back, to a wooden post in the middle of the cave, the ropes binding them glowing with magical energy. Thirty or more people in dark-red robes stood around them, their faces covered by hoods. On the front of their robes was the same upside-down skull symbol that they'd all seen on the screen back at headquarters. Then, it had made Denzel uncomfortable. Here and now, it terrified him.

"It's some sort of cult," Smithy whispered.

The figures swayed slowly, making rhythmical movements with their hands as they chanted the same repetitive words over and over.

Naga-raxuk koonto shah. Naga-raxuk koonto shah.

Denzel wanted to ask Tabatha if she knew what the words meant, but he was too terrified to speak. If they were really lucky, it would turn out to mean: "Sorry about this, we've made a terrible mistake, feel free to leave at any time."

But he suspected no one was *that* lucky, and especially not him.

Tabatha prodded him with her cane, getting his attention, then pointed to a raised area of the floor that almost looked like a stage. It was closer to the tunnel mouth than Samara and Boyle were, and Denzel had to shuffle forward on his elbows a little to see it properly.

A tall figure in a purple robe stood in silence on the raised area, facing the centre of the cave. He held a long golden staff in one hand, the bottom resting on the floor, a half-moon-shaped blade pointing towards the ceiling. Denzel guessed this guy must be the leader from the way he nodded his approval at the chanting.

Naga-raxuk koonto shah. Naga-raxuk koonto shah.

There was something beside the man in purple that Denzel could see from the corner of his eye. When he looked directly at it, though, it disappeared. He focused on the leader and tried to let his peripheral vision figure out what else was down there with him.

It was a person, he thought, although it was hard to say for sure. It felt a bit like looking at a Magic Eye picture, where you had to look through the image rather than at it in order for the real picture to be revealed.

Denzel shifted his gaze to the spot where the figure was and tried to focus on the floor beyond it. The air trembled as if alive.

Naga-raxuk koonto shah. Naga-raxuk koonto shah.

"What's that?" Denzel whispered. He pointed to the spot where he could almost see the shape, but Tabatha and Smithy just stared blankly down at it.

"The ground," said Smithy. "Why do you ask?"

Denzel shook his head. "There's something there," he insisted, squinting to try to bring it into focus. "I can see ... something."

He was still squinting when he realised that the cave had fallen silent. The chanting had stopped. In the sudden quiet that followed, Denzel was sure his crashing heartbeat would give them away. He held his breath, terrified, waiting to see what would happen next.

The robed figures had stopped chanting, but they continued to sway gently from side to side. At the centre of the circle, Boyle and Samara squirmed and struggled against their restraints. Denzel could hear Samara muttering various incantations, but whatever magic had enchanted the ropes was proving too powerful for her to break.

"We've been expecting you."

The voice rose up suddenly from the figure in purple. The robed figures all turned and raised their heads in the direction of the tunnel mouth.

Smithy shot Denzel a worried look. "He's not talking to us, is he?"

Denzel swallowed. "I think he probably is, yeah."

"Do not keep us waiting, Denzel."

Denzel nodded. His voice came as a low croak. "Yeah. Definitely us."

The next voice that rose up to the tunnel was Boyle's. It was shrill and urgent, more scared than Denzel had ever heard it.

"Denzel, run!"

The panic in Boyle's voice kicked Denzel into life. He jumped to his feet and turned to run, only for a tiny golden hand to grab him by the bottom of his trousers.

He tripped, fell and *thudded* hard against the rocky floor.

"Sorry, kid," said Tabatha, drawing herself up to her full height. She pressed a foot on Smithy's back, holding him down, then twirled her cane and pointed it at Denzel. The finger extended like a little gun. "You two aren't going anywhere."

CHAPTER 7

For the third time in the past few minutes, Denzel found himself being pulled through solid rock. Tabatha released her grip on him as they all emerged on to the raised platform, sending him stumbling over the edge and crashing to the floor. As he fell, he disturbed the air, making hundreds of candles all around the cavern flicker and dance.

Denzel looked up to find himself surrounded by hooded figures. Smithy landed in a heap beside him, a wounded expression on his face.

"Wait, you're a *bad guy*?" Smithy gasped, turning in time to see Tabatha jumping down from the stage behind him. "How can you be a bad guy? You said you were a good guy!"

"I said I was *sometimes* good," Tabatha corrected. "And sometimes bad. Today, I'm bad."

She smiled sweetly and winked at him.

"If it's any consolation, I think you're cute."

Smithy huffed and stammered out a random series of disconnected words and noises. "Well! That's! I'm! Sheesh! So! Hmm! Now! But!"

He put his hands on his hips, nodded firmly a couple of times, then sort of deflated with a sigh. "I want a divorce."

Denzel sprang to his feet and spun around, taking in their surroundings. He quickly tried to calculate how many of the robed figures he could successfully take in a fight, and decided that the answer was almost certainly "none". That was a problem.

Tabatha had betrayed them. That was also a problem.

Boyle and Samara were tied up. Another one for the problem column.

And then there was the figure in the purple robe, and the shimmering shape that was barely visible beside him. Those were also problems.

A giant version of the upside-down skull was carved into the wall directly above the leader's head. Denzel's stomach tightened in fear at the sight of it, and he decided he may as well lump that in with all the other problems too.

All things considered, then, things were not looking positive.

"Who are you?" Denzel asked.

"Ask them what they want," Smithy suggested.

"What do you want?" Denzel asked.

"Ask them if they're going to kill us," Smithy whispered.

"Are you going to— Wait. You're already dead," Denzel replied.

"Oh! Yeah!" Smithy said, brightening. He wiped a hand across his brow. "Phew! That's a relief. Ask them if they're going to kill you."

The golden hand of Tabatha's cane appeared between their heads. She flicked her wrist and the hand slapped them both on the face, one after another.

"Ow!" Denzel protested.

"That's just mean," said Smithy.

From behind them, they heard Boyle growl. "I knew it. I knew we couldn't trust her."

"You could have said something," Smithy sniffed.

"I did!" Boyle snapped. "I said, 'I don't trust her.'"

Denzel nodded. "He did say that."

Smithy blinked. "Oh. Right. Well, fair enough then." He

gave the helpless Boyle a thumbs-up. "Good job."

"Silence!" boomed the figure in purple.

All around the cave, the word came again as whispers from beneath the hoods.

"Silence."

"Silence."

"Silence."

"Who are you?" asked the cult leader. It was a man's voice and he spoke in a strange stilted sort of way that suggested he didn't often speak English.

Denzel frowned. "You know who I am. You called me Denzel a minute ago."

The cult leader's head turned a fraction towards him. "I wasn't talking to you. I was talking to her."

"Oh. Sorry," said Denzel. "With the hood up it makes it hard to..." His voice died away. He cleared his throat. "I'll shut up now."

"Tabatha Tarrin," said Tabatha, taking a bow. "Spectre at large. I thought I'd help you guys out by bringing you this one."

She tapped Denzel on the head with her cane.

"Why?" asked the cult leader.

Tabatha twirled her cane and pointed it up at the carving above the leader's head. "Because of that."

Denzel and Smithy both turned to look at her. "Wait,

you know what that is?" Denzel asked.

The golden hand slapped them both across the face again. "Shh. Grown-ups talking," Tabatha instructed.

"You serve Him?" the man in the purple robe asked. Beside him, Denzel was sure he saw the indistinct shape take a step closer. He shifted his gaze to it and tried to figure out what it was.

Man-sized. Definitely man-sized. Legs, he thought. Possibly arms too. If he really squinted, there was something on top that might be a head, but might equally be a big turnip.

"I'd like to," said Tabatha, shrugging. "I've spent years trying to track Him down, and now I've found you guys, I thought I'd seize my chance."

The cult leader regarded her from beneath his hood. "I see," he said, after some consideration. "And you thought you could earn a place among us by bringing us the Chosen One?"

The same confused expression settled on the faces of Denzel, Smithy, Samara and Boyle.

"Chosen One?" said Samara.

"Who's the Chosen One?" asked Denzel.

He looked around at the others to find them all staring back at him in surprise.

"Who is it?" he asked again.

Smithy looked his friend up and down. "I'll give you three guesses," he said. "And the first two don't count."

Denzel's lips moved silently, as if attempting a tricky maths calculation in his head. After a few seconds of this, his eyebrows raised almost all the way to his hairline.

"Wait, *me*? I'm the Chosen One?" he gasped. "Chosen by who? For what? How? Why? When?"

He tried to think of some more questions to ask, but decided those pretty much covered everything. He could've gone for "Where?" he supposed, but it felt unnecessary.

The cult leader's voice became an awestruck whisper. "For thousands of years, we have waited, we followers of the Cult of Shantankar. We have existed since the beginning. Since the First."

"The first what?" Boyle demanded.

"The first ghost," the leader said. A shudder of excitement passed through him, making the bottom of his robe swish. "Since the Ghostfather."

All around the cave, the hooded figures dipped their heads and bowed. From the corner of his eye, Denzel thought he saw the blurry shape beside the cult leader bow too. For a moment, it became more solid, and Denzel caught a glimpse of ornate red armour and black hair tied back in a tight bun before it vanished again.

"Who's the Ghostfather when he's at home?" Smithy wondered.

"Legend says he was the first ever ghost," said Samara. "The original supernatural entity to walk the Earth."

"A real big bad," Boyle added. "The worst of them all. But it's a legend. A fairy story."

"It is no fairytale, I assure you," said the cult leader, his voice becoming hard and cold. "The Ghostfather is very real. And soon, with the help of the Chosen One, He shall return. We will use the key to open the lock, and then, at last, He shall come back."

The whispers rose up around the cave.

"He is coming."

"He is coming."

"He is coming."

"And when the Ghostfather walks the Earth once more, all shall tremble before Him."

Smithy stepped forward and puffed up his chest. "Denzel will *never* help you!"

"Right!" agreed Denzel.

"He'd rather die!"

"Er, yes," Denzel said, sounding slightly less convinced.

"He'd rather have his guts ripped out through his eyes and his bones ground into a paste than help you lot!"

"Well..." Denzel began, shifting uncomfortably.

"He'd rather have all his skin flayed off him and his insides boiled in oil, then have a hot metal spike rammed—"

"I think they get the point," Denzel squeaked. He cleared his throat and tried to disguise the shake in his voice. "Smithy's right. I won't help you."

"Oh, Denzel," said the cult leader. Although they couldn't see his face, they could hear the smile in his voice. "You already have."

He gestured to Tabatha. "Bring him to me. Show your loyalty."

Tabatha nodded. "OK. But first, let me just check I got everything." She began counting on her fingers. "Cult of Shantankar, Ghostfather, Chosen One, blah-blah-blah, evil plan, rule the world, et cetera, et cetera."

She beamed broadly at the cult leader. "Yep. I think that's all we need for now."

Leaping sideways, Tabatha caught Boyle and Samara by their arms and pulled. The Spectre Collectors became see-through for a moment and slipped out from the ropes that had been binding them to the stake.

"What? What is the meaning of this?" demanded the cult leader.

"What does it look like, hood guy?" Tabatha asked. She flicked her wrist and her cane went spinning behind her. It hit one of the robed figures with a *clonk*, dropping him to the floor, then returned to her hand. "It's a break-out!"

Smithy thrust both hands into the air and cheered. "And the wedding is *back on!*"

Denzel ducked as a jet of flame erupted from Samara's fingers, sending cult members scurrying for cover. Boyle lunged after one and brought him down with a well-aimed kick to the back of the leg. He spun and blocked as another of the cultists grabbed for him, then used the man's own momentum to send him crashing into two more of the hooded figures.

"Raaaaargh!"

The cult leader ran at Denzel, his arms raised, his fingers clawing at the air. Denzel danced on the spot in panic. Chaos had broken out all around him, and there was no way he could jump out of the leader's path in time.

He was bracing himself for the impact when Smithy barrelled into the leader, sending them both crashing to the floor.

"I've got him! I've got him!" Smithy yelped, sitting on the man's head and squashing it against the floor.

"Get off me!" the leader spat. He flailed wildly, but Smithy kicked and slapped at his hands, stopping him from being able to get a hold.

Tabatha came bounding between Smithy and Denzel. They watched as she delivered a flying kick to one of the cultists, then somersaulted over him and brought her cane down on the head of another robed figure behind the first.

Smithy grinned at Denzel and gave him a wink. "See? I knew she wasn't a bad guy."

Denzel was about to reply when the thing on the stage came into focus, and he finally saw it for what it was. A tall woman with dark hair and narrow eyes stood there, her polished red armour glinting in the glow of the candlelight.

As Denzel watched, she drew a long Samurai sword from a scabbard on her belt, and twirled it in a way that suggested she not only knew how to use it, but would take great pleasure in demonstrating that fact.

"Um..." said Denzel, as the woman's eyes locked on his.

He turned to look for help, but Samara, Boyle and Tabatha were all busy fighting the hooded figures, and Smithy was wriggling his bottom on the leader's head and laughing.

Just before he turned back, Denzel saw a second woman in red appear across the cave. Even over the sounds of the fighting and Smithy's laughter, he heard the *shinkt* of her sword being drawn.

Shinkt.

Shinkt.

Shinkt.

The sound came from all around him. More and more of the armoured women appeared, their eyes immediately fixing on Denzel as they drew their long, slender blades. Denzel turned slowly on the spot, trying to count them all. There were ten at least, perhaps more. One by one, they all moved towards him, closing in from all sides.

"Uh, guys!" Denzel cried. "We have a problem!"

He turned in time to find a blade slicing towards him, but not nearly in enough time to avoid it. Instead, he could only screw his eyes shut and brace himself as the sword *whummed* through the air.

And then, with a *clank*, it stopped. Denzel opened one eye to find Boyle blocking the sword with his arm. The blade had sliced through his uniform, revealing scuffed metal plating beneath it.

With his other arm, Boyle shoved Denzel in the chest, sending him stumbling backwards. "Get out of here," he barked.

Denzel watched in horror as the Samurai spun on her heel and arced her sword around. Boyle ducked, and the blade scythed just millimetres above his head. He spun into a sweeping kick, but his leg passed harmlessly through the intangible figure.

Off-balance, there was nowhere for Boyle to go when the Samurai raised her sword above her head and brought it slicing down towards him.

A bolt of magical energy slammed into her, launching her backwards across the cave. Denzel turned to see Samara standing behind him, her fingertips crackling with magical power. All around her, the other Samurai closed in.

"Look out!" Denzel warned, but Samara didn't turn. Instead, she raised a hand and took aim at his chest.

"Run," she whispered.

And then, as one of the Samurai-ghosts launched herself at her, Samara fired a glowing bolt of blue energy in Denzel's direction, and the world unspooled around him.

CHAPTER 8

The world stopped spinning a few seconds later. Denzel, however, did not.

He screamed as he tumbled through darkness, yelped when he bounced on something wet and slightly squishy, then babbled incoherently when he went rolling down a grassy hillside.

At last, after what felt like forever, he slammed into a tree and came to a sudden, jarring stop.

Denzel didn't think he had ever been grateful for smashing face-first into a tree before, but he'd been starting to worry that he was never going to stop, so this particular tree was a welcome one. Heaving himself up on its bottom branches, he had a quick check for broken bones, then tried to figure out where he was.

Wherever it was, it was dark, grassy, mountainous, and rainy.

Still Scotland then.

Night had drawn in, and the blanket of cloud cover turned the light from the moon into a faint patch of white on the grey ceiling above. He'd lost his torch in the cave somewhere. He couldn't remember where, and reckoned it didn't really matter. He didn't have it now, and that was the main thing.

Cupping his hands above his eyes to shield them from the rain, he looked back up the hillside he'd come rolling down. He couldn't see the cave entrance anywhere. He couldn't see any landmarks he recognised, in fact, unless you counted puddles.

Down the hill wasn't any better. There were a few trees scattered around, the edges of their leaves reflecting the thin moonlight. For a moment, he thought he saw a light somewhere down near the bottom of the slope, but then the rain lashed at his face again, forcing him to turn away.

It was then that he heard it – a sudden movement in the foliage behind him. He spun on the spot, punching wildly at the air, but finding nothing. For the briefest of seconds, he thought the sound must've been his imagination, but then an ominous white shape appeared from behind a clump of bushes, and bleak, doleful eyes gazed deep into his own.

Baaaaa.

Denzel leaned against the tree and exhaled. "You almost gave me a heart attack," he whispered.

The sheep stared back at him, its mouth moving as it thoughtfully chewed on some grass.

Baaaaa, another sheep chimed in from a little distance away. This one was munching on a clump of weeds that sprouted from a puddle of mud.

"Easy for you to say," Denzel told it. "You're not the one being chased by—"

Both sheep suddenly shot off down the hill, their feet thundering across the grass and mud. One of them glanced back briefly, its eyes bulging in terror as it stared past Denzel at the hillside above.

Denzel saw them then, three red-clad shapes coming bounding down the hillside, their swords drawn. They'd found him. The Samurai-ghosts had found him.

For a few seconds, Denzel flapped in panic and considered his options. He thought about climbing the tree, but it was only about ten feet tall, and it didn't have many leaves to hide in.

He thought about standing his ground and fighting.

That thought didn't last long.

With a high-pitched "Wait for me!" Denzel threw himself down the hillside after the sheep. He ran in big, bounding steps, gravity dragging him along just as much as his legs were propelling him. He tripped and stumbled, skidded and slipped, spiralling his arms around in terror as his momentum grew and his legs were forced to run faster and faster to stop himself falling.

The grass and mud became slippery stone shale that was not unlike loose gravel. Denzel's out-of-control run became an even more out-of-control slide, and he hurtled down, down, down the darkened hillside, picking up speed with every second that passed.

On the one hand, this was good. He was confident that he had to be going faster than the ghosts, which meant he would be pulling ahead.

On the other hand, he would presumably reach the bottom eventually, and he wasn't sure what would happen then. At this speed, and with no means of slowing down, he was pretty confident it wouldn't be anything good.

He didn't have long to wait to find out. The hillside levelled off suddenly, and Denzel's downward slide became a frantic forward stagger. In the darkness, he saw the ground fall away just ahead of him, and realised with a sinking feeling that he was going to run right off a cliff in five more steps.

Unfortunately, he realised this four steps in, and the final step found nothing but thin air. Denzel fell straight down, his arms flapping, his legs kicking furiously at nothing but empty space. His mouth opened as if to scream, but before he could utter a sound he slammed into a big rock that stuck out from the cliff face, knocking all the air out of him in one painfully brief wheeze.

After the rock came a tree, then another tree, then a second rock, and then a series of increasingly large branches. And then, after all that, came the ground. It was quite soft, as ground went, thanks mostly to the rain. The various branches and rocks had all slowed his fall too, so that when he finally hit the ground he sort of *schlopped* into it without doing himself any more damage than he already had.

Groaning, he tried to stand, but his body made it clear that it wasn't ready for that yet, *thank you very much*, and he had no choice but to lie there in the soggy darkness, waiting for his breath to return.

As he waited, Denzel saw three shapes moving above him. He held his breath and watched as the pursuing Samurai-ghosts went sailing above the treetops and vanished into the darkness ahead.

He kept holding his breath for as long as he could, before finally letting it out in one long, soft gasp.

They hadn't seen him. The ghosts hadn't seen him! He'd lost them. He was safe. For now, at least. He started to sit up, then stopped himself.

What if they came back? Or what if this was a trick and they were waiting on the other side of the tree, ready to slice him into several different pieces the moment he got to his feet?

He lay back down and decided to wait where he was for a little longer, just to be absolutely sure that the coast was clear. Three or four hours should do it.

Half a day, tops.

Two and a half minutes later, Denzel was so cold and wet that he reckoned being sliced into variously sized bits would be preferable. He pulled himself out of the mud and spent a few moments listening for any sign that he'd been spotted.

When he was confident that no one was about to swing a sword at him, he set himself to figuring out what he should do next. The cliff face behind him was too steep to climb, even with the rocky outcrops he'd thumped into on the way down. He might be able to climb one of the trees, but even if he reached the top he'd have to jump a large gap in pitch darkness, with the wind howling around him.

He didn't much fancy that.

If he walked away from the cliff, he'd be following the Samurai-ghosts, which didn't strike him as a very sensible idea.

That left two directions, both of which ran parallel to the cliff. Neither one seemed any more promising than the other, so he picked one and started walking.

Then he changed his mind, turned round and walked the other way instead.

As he walked, he worried. He worried about Smithy, Samara, Tabatha and Boyle, more or less in that order. He worried about the Cult of Shantankar, and about the Ghostfather. He worried for a good few minutes about the whole "Chosen One" thing, and the idea that he would somehow be responsible for unleashing an ancient evil upon the Earth.

That would be a bummer.

The more he walked, the more worried Denzel became about something else. Something more pressing than Chosen Ones or Ghostfathers.

"Yep," he sighed, stopping beneath a tree and taking shelter beneath its branches. "I'm completely lost."

And he was. On his left, the cliff face had become a

sloping hillside that was still far too steep to climb. On his right, a few metres of grass and bracken gave way to absolute darkness that he couldn't possibly see anything through.

The rain had changed from a sideways torrent to a steady downpour of large, fat drops that *plinked* on the leaves overhead. Even if he called for help, no one would hear him, with the possible exception of the Samurai-ghosts.

He could have navigated using the stars, were it not for the fact that they were hidden by the clouds. And, more importantly, for the fact that he had no idea how.

The rain had found its way inside his jacket and was soaking him to the skin now. As he stood there all alone in the darkness, Denzel began to shiver. Or maybe he'd been shivering for a while. The cold and the rain made it hard to think straight.

The wind whistled around him, making him colder still. He couldn't stay out here. If he didn't find cover soon, he wouldn't have to worry about the Samurai-ghosts killing him – the gathering storm would do it for them.

There had to be somewhere he could go. There had to be somewhere he could hide until the weather and the ghosts had moved on. But where?

As if in answer to that question, a fork of lightning tore

across the dark night sky, briefly painting the landscape in its electric glow.

For a moment, Denzel thought he saw a ramshackle old house just a couple of hundred metres down the hillside, and then the darkness returned to swallow it up.

He fixed his gaze on the spot where he thought he'd seen it, and began an unsteady limp in that direction. Several times he tripped and stumbled, but he daren't look down, daren't take his eyes off the patch of darkness ahead of him. If he lost track of where the house was now, he might never find it again.

Another bolt of lightning cracked the night wide open, revealing a run-down old cottage that seemed to slouch on its foundations as if too tired to stand upright. Moss grew across the whitewashed stone walls. The garden was a tangle of weeds and grass, somehow even more unkempt than the wilderness around him.

But it had walls and a roof, which meant he could shelter there. Probably not until the rain went off – he didn't think the rain was ever going to go off – but at least until morning.

He was halfway along the path when the door opened. He'd assumed the house was abandoned, and so he let out a little gasp of fright when the door creaked slowly inward on its hinges and a figure in a long white nightdress appeared, the light from a candle she held showing off a road map of wrinkles on her face.

"Now, what in the name o' the wee man are you doing out in this weather?" the old woman asked him. She stepped aside and beckoned him into the darkened hallway. "Come away in, before you catch your death..."

CHAPTER 9

The inside of the house was not as tired and ramshackle as the outside.

It was worse.

Patches of damp bloomed across the wallpaper that hung in peeling strips from the living-room wall. Slimy-looking mushrooms sprouted from a carpet, the original colour of which was lost beneath a layer of grime. Most of the furniture was caked with dust, except for a sideboard over by the window, which was covered in hundreds of dead flies.

All things considered, Denzel would've preferred to take his chances outside.

"Wild out there, the night," said the old woman, as if reading his mind. Her voice was soft, with an unmistakable Scottish brogue that would normally have set Denzel at ease, had it not been for everything else going on.

She used her candle to light another two at opposite ends of the room, and crooked shadows were chased across the walls. The candlelight picked out the lines of her wrinkles and made her eyes blaze. "You're lucky you found me."

Denzel glanced around at the filthy room. The smell was snagging at the back of his throat and he was trying very hard not to throw up on the carpet. Not that it would've made it any worse.

"I'm Mrs Gourlay," the woman said, smiling to reveal a complete lack of teeth. She gestured to him with a frail, skinny hand. "And who might you be?"

"Uh, I'm Denzel," he replied, his eyes darting to the door. The house was making his skin crawl, and something about the woman was giving him the heebie-jeebies. He should've stayed outside and taken his chances in the wind and the rain. At least out there he wasn't at risk of catching the plague.

"Denzel!" said Mrs Gourlay. "A fine name, for a fine young man, I'm sure."

A shocked expression crossed her face. "Oh! But where

are my manners? Would you like a wee cup of tea?"

Denzel's eyes darted to the mushrooms and dead flies. He daren't even imagine what the kitchen would be like.

"Er, no, I'm fine. Thanks."

Mrs Gourlay nodded. "Just as well. I'm all out of teabags and I'm pretty sure the milk's on the turn." She shooed him towards one of the musty armchairs. "Sit down! Sit down! Before you make the place look untidy."

Denzel wanted to say he thought that ship had probably already sailed, but then thought that might be rude. He didn't really want to sit down either, though. In fact, the longer he spent in the house, the greater his urge to get out became.

"I should probably be going, actually," he said. "My friends are waiting for me."

He made a move to the door but Mrs Gourlay was there before him. She closed it with a slam, blocking the way to the hall. "I can't let you do that, I'm afraid," she told him. The old woman smiled in a way that seemed overly friendly, like she was trying too hard. "It's far too dangerous to be roaming around on a night like this. No. Just you stay here with me until it's safe."

Denzel felt the fine hairs on the back of his neck stand up. "My friends will be coming."

Mrs Gourlay shook her head slowly. "No, Denzel. They

won't. No one's coming for you. No one friendly, at any rate."

Denzel swallowed. The woman was slight and frail, and he was reasonably confident he could push her out of the way if he had to. Then again, what sort of monster would he be if he started shoving pensioners around just because they were a little bit creepy?

She grinned broadly, showing her empty gums.

OK, a *lot* creepy.

"You're right. I'd better stay here," he agreed. "But, uh, can I use the bathroom?"

Mrs Gourlay's eyes narrowed a fraction. "The bathroom?" she said, glancing briefly at the closed door behind her.

"Um, yeah," said Denzel, dancing on the spot for effect. "I really need to go."

For a while, the old woman said nothing, and Denzel was sure she was about to see through his plan. Eventually, though, she nodded and handed him the candle. "Second on the left," she said, opening the living-room door and ushering him through. "I'll wait outside. You know, in case you have any trouble."

"I'm sure I'll be fine," said Denzel, shuffling into the hallway and towards the bathroom door. In truth, he was terrified of what he might find in there. The living room and hall were both horrifying, but the bathroom had the potential to be several magnitudes worse. Still, it would be worth it if it gave him a chance to escape.

"Nonsense," said Mrs Gourlay, following behind him. She stopped when they reached the bathroom. "I'll be waiting right here."

Denzel shuffled backwards into the bathroom, too scared to look at it yet. The walls in the hall were just as filthy and rotten as those in the living room, and the carpet had either worn away or been eaten by bugs. Possibly both.

Mrs Gourlay took a step closer, and at first Denzel thought she was following him in, but then she caught the door handle and pulled the door closed between them. It closed with a *clunk*, and Denzel immediately slid closed the little lock that was fitted to the rotting wood.

That done, he took a moment to compose himself, then turned to find out what horrors awaited him in the bathroom.

After some consideration, he had to admit that it wasn't quite as bad as he thought. It wasn't far off, but it wasn't *quite* as stomach-churningly terrible as he'd been expecting. Sure, the walls and ceiling were stained with blacks and browns, and the linoleum had mostly rotted away beneath his feet, but the toilet itself was reasonably clean, and nothing like the horror show he had been bracing himself for.

The ceiling above the bath had sprung a leak at some point in the dim and distant past, and had partially collapsed, covering the inside of the tub with plaster, dust and a mulchy dark goo. A little rubber duck was half buried in it, one eye and part of a beak poking out. The eye seemed to gaze hopefully at Denzel, but there was no way he was reaching his hand into that lot to rescue it.

To Denzel's great relief, the bathroom had a window. It wasn't huge, but big enough for him to climb through, and easily accessible if he stood on the toilet lid and clambered up on to the windowsill.

"Everything all right in there?" asked Mrs Gourlay, her voice coming from right on the other side of the door.

"Fine!" said Denzel. "I'll just be a minute."

Slipping his hand up inside his sleeve so he didn't have to touch the toilet directly, he quietly lowered the white plastic lid and climbed up on to the cistern. From there, he was able to lean across and reach the window latch. The metal was old and rusted, but with a few hard tugs he was able to unlock it.

That was where things got tricky. Although the latch was off, the window had been painted shut, and refused to budge. Gritting his teeth and leaning closer to the glass, Denzel tried to force the window upwards in its frame. He just needed to move it fifty centimetres or so, and he'd be able to climb out. That was all. Half a metre, probably even less.

Rain battered against the pane from outside. Denzel had placed the candle on the windowsill while he tried to wrestle the window into submission, and a distorted version of his own face reflected back at him in the glass.

There was a faint *creak* as the window budged half a centimetre upwards. Denzel almost cheered. Getting it started was always going to be the problem. Now that he'd broken the paint seal, it should be much easier to—

"What are you doing, Denzel?"

Mrs Gourlay's voice came from the other side of the glass. Denzel froze as her face appeared outside, the thin candlelight dancing across her withered features, the rain matting her grey hair to her forehead.

The sight of her kicked Denzel into full-scale panic mode. He stumbled backwards, fell off the toilet and landed with a *thud* on the rotten floor. Kicking and scrabbling to his feet, he threw himself at the bathroom door. As he hit it, the rotten wood immediately collapsed and he went stumbling across the narrow hallway.

There was another door there. Denzel threw it open, staggered inside and hurriedly closed it behind him. He leaned against it for a few moments, catching his breath, and then turned to survey the room he found himself in.

And that was when he found the skeleton.

It lay propped up on a double bed, its empty eye sockets watching the door. Beside it, there was a bedside table, on which sat a set of knitting needles and a ball of wool, a cup and saucer, and a little glass with a set of false teeth inside.

Denzel's eyes were dragged back to the skeleton. He couldn't see much of the nightdress it wore, but he could see enough to recognise it. It wasn't difficult. He'd seen it just a moment before, through the window.

The wall beside the bed rippled, and Mrs Gourlay stepped through. Denzel babbled in panic, then some primal part of him decided babbling wasn't enough, and he launched into a full-on scream.

Mrs Gourlay seemed to teleport across the room. One moment she was over by the skeleton, the next she was standing in front of him. A withered hand clamped across his mouth. Cold radiated from it, stinging his skin and making him shiver.

"Hold your wheesht, now," the old woman whispered. "What are you trying to do, wake the dead?"

Her eyes widened. A gummy grin almost split her face in two. "Because, if so, you're a wee bit too late..."

CHAPTER 10

Denzel stared. There wasn't much more he could do. Mrs Gourlay still had one hand clamped across his mouth and was gripping his arm with the other, stopping him getting away.

She hadn't stopped smiling at him, but if it was intended to put him at ease, it was having exactly the opposite effect. Denzel's stomach was stuck somewhere in his chest, and his heart was currently thumping inside his head. He wanted to scream and run, not necessarily in that order. Unfortunately, the icy-cold grip of Mrs Gourlay prevented him doing either.

"Now, don't you worry, I'm not going to hurt

you," the old woman said.

Denzel wanted to point out that the way she was clutching his arm was actually hurting quite a lot, but the hand on his mouth and the terror in his throat prevented him.

"I've been waiting a long time for you, Denzel," Mrs Gourlay continued. Her milky eyes scanned his face, as if taking in every detail. "I have to admit, though, you're not what I expected. You're awfully short for a Chosen One."

She glanced at the room around them, paused briefly on the skeleton, then regarded the window. A set of heavy curtains had long ago been drawn across it. They hung limply, the bottoms frayed from where mice had nibbled at them.

"Right, I'm going to take my hand away," Mrs Gourlay told him. "If you scream it'll only delay things, and we don't have a lot of time. Got it?"

Denzel tried to nod, but the old woman's hand was like a vice on his head. He managed a muffled, "Mm-hmmf" instead.

"Good lad," said Mrs Gourlay. "I'm trusting you. I hope you'll trust me too."

She released her grip and stepped back. Denzel's legs twitched, trying to carry him to the door, but the rest of him missed their signal and he ended up just doing a little panicky dance on the spot.

"You're... You're..."

"Dead. Aye," said Mrs Gourlay.

"And you're a... You're a..."

"Ghost. That's right." She winked at him. "No fooling you, is there?"

Denzel was absolutely sure that he had a lot of questions he wanted to ask. It was just that, at this particular moment, he was too scared to think of any. Only one occurred to him, and he didn't think it was particularly useful.

He asked it anyway.

"What happened?"

Mrs Gourlay looked over to the skeleton. Her smile faded, becoming something much sadder.

"You know, I can barely remember. It was a long time ago," she said. "But it was peaceful, which is about all we can really ask for."

She shook her head, then turned back to him, her smile returning. "But we're not here to talk about me. We've much more important matters to discuss."

"We do?" Denzel whispered. "L-like what?"

"Like the Ghostfather, and the end of the world," said Mrs Gourlay. "And what you're going to do about it."

Denzel's mouth opened and closed a few times, like he was trying to speak but the words weren't coming out.

"Whatever you're trying to say, I'm sure it's very interesting. But I'm afraid I can't hang around for you to get it out," said Mrs Gourlay. Her eyes darted up to the ceiling, as if she'd heard something moving up there. "We're up against the clock."

"Why? What's going on?" Denzel whispered.

"First thing's first. You are the Chosen One, right?" Mrs Gourlay asked. "I'd hate to have got the wrong lad."

Denzel shifted uncomfortably, then nodded. "Yeah. I mean, I think so. I mean, that's what the weirdos in the robes said."

"Och, that's marvellous! Good for you, son," said Mrs Gourlay. She gave him a friendly jab on the shoulder, which almost knocked him off his feet. For the size of her, she was surprisingly strong.

"Thanks," said Denzel. "But I didn't really do anything."

"*Yet*," the old woman corrected. "You didn't really do anything *yet*. But you will. Aye, you will."

Denzel scratched his head, a little embarrassed by the way Mrs Gourlay was staring at him. "Who is he, anyway? The Ghostfather?"

Mrs Gourlay sucked in her bottom lip. "Aye, they said you'd ask that. Told me what I should do about it when you did." She shook her head. "I told them I wasn't keen though. It seems awfully cruel."

"What does?" Denzel asked.

The old woman lunged, clamped both hands on either side of his head, and held him there like she was about to give him a big sloppy kiss.

"This," she said, and then the room flipped upside down and poured like sand into Denzel's brain.

Denzel stood high on a barren hillside, red clouds writhing in the dark sky above him. From up here, he could see what felt like the whole world. He saw cities, countries, continents, all crumbling and burning.

He saw oceans boiling, lakes freezing, and rivers running red with blood. He heard screams and wails and desperate, hopeless cries. They rose up from everywhere at once, filling his head until he too wanted to scream with them.

A fork of lightning cracked the sky apart, and Denzel saw it. No, not it. *Him*. He had no shape, and yet every shape. He emerged from the shattered sky, too large for Denzel to be able to comprehend, and yet too small to see with the naked eye.

Denzel's brain itched as it tried to process all this conflicting information, and then the shapeless nothingness became a hulking figure that looked to have been carved from a chunk of solid darkness.

Only it wasn't darkness. Not really. It was more than that. The figure was made from a complete absence of light. It was as if a mountain-sized, man-shaped hole had been torn in the universe.

A mountain-sized, man-shaped hole that walked towards Denzel, his feet burning the world where he stepped.

Denzel was frozen to the spot in fear. He couldn't move a muscle. Even if he could, where would he go? There was nowhere safe from this thing. Nowhere on Earth, and maybe nowhere beyond it either.

The figure stopped beside the hill and leaned down until his face was level with Denzel's. He had no obvious mouth, yet he spoke with a voice that turned the rocks around Denzel to dust and filled him with a crushing sense of utter despair.

"I am coming," he said.

And with that, the world imploded.

"Wh-what was that?" Denzel babbled, falling to the floor, his eyes darting around the decaying bedroom. "What did you do to me?"

"I'm sorry. I really am," said Mrs Gourlay. "They said it

was the only way you'd understand. I had to show you."

Denzel spent almost a minute trying to bring his breathing back under control before he spoke again.

"That was him, wasn't it? That was the Ghostfather."

"Aye," Mrs Gourlay said. "That was him."

"Who is he?" asked Denzel, getting shakily to his feet. "*What* is he?"

"Something ancient. Something evil," said Mrs Gourlay. "They say he was the first ghost, born of rage and hatred. They tell me he almost destroyed the world of the living before they were able to banish him. If he comes back..."

She looked scared for a moment, but then smiled and shook her head. "Well. He won't. You won't let him. You'll stop him. And I'm going to help you!"

She dashed across the room, reached her hands through the top of a chest of drawers and began rummaging around inside.

"See, the Elders gave me a job to do. They asked me to keep watch out for you. They said you'd turn up one day, didn't say how or when, just that you'd show up, and that I was to help you."

Denzel's brow furrowed. "The Spectre Collector Elders?"

Mrs Gourlay let out a little cackle. "Och, no. Much

older than those eejits. The Ghost Elders."

"Ghost Elders?" Denzel said. "Who are they? Since when were there Ghost Elders?"

"Since always," said Mrs Gourlay. "Well, for a long time, anyway. Long before your little club."

Denzel didn't think Samara and Boyle would be happy to hear the Spectre Collectors described as a "little club" but decided not to say anything.

"Aha! Here we are!"

Mrs Gourlay turned away from the chest of drawers and held up a garish gold necklace with a chunky chain and a skull pendant hanging from it.

In a blink, the old woman appeared at Denzel's side again. She thrust the necklace eagerly into his hands. "They told me to give you this."

Denzel looked down at the necklace. He'd be the first to admit that he was no expert on jewellery, but he knew what he liked. And he did *not* like this thing. It looked like something a gangsta rapper would wear, complementing it with a set of gold teeth.

"What am I supposed to do with it?" he asked.

"Well, wear it, of course!"

Denzel was afraid she might say that. "Wear it?" he groaned. "Seriously? Why?"

"I don't know," Mrs Gourlay admitted. "But they said it

was awfully important."

"Who? The Ghost Elders?"

"You catch on fast," said Mrs Gourlay, shooting him a gummy smile. "And before you ask, no, I don't know how they knew you'd turn up at my door."

Denzel hadn't even thought about that. Now that he had, he was more confused than ever.

"How *did* they know?" he wondered.

"Like I say, I haven't a clue. They seemed pretty sure you'd show up some day, though," Mrs Gourlay said. "They also told me to say…"

She looked up, as if struggling to remember something. "*Follow this the*… No, wait, that's not it. *Wherever this goes*…"

She frowned and scratched her head. "No. No. *Something something pendant follows.*"

"Was the *something something* bit important?" Denzel asked.

"Aye, probably," Mrs Gourlay admitted. She shrugged. "I can't remember the exact wording, but it basically said that this should follow the Ghostfather."

Denzel looked down at the pendant again. The hollow eyes of the skull stared blankly back up at him. "How can it follow the Ghostfather?"

"I have no idea. That's all I know. You need to wear it,

and it should follow the Ghostfather."

"So *I* need to follow the Ghostfather?"

"Maybe," said Mrs Gourlay. "I mean, it's no' got any legs of its own, so I suppose that must be it. All I know is I've waited years to give that to someone, so I really hope you're the right lad."

Denzel hoped he wasn't, but didn't say as much. "Years?"

"Decades, probably!" Mrs Gourlay replied. "Probably. I lose track. What century is this?"

"Twenty-first," said Denzel.

"It never is!" the old woman gasped. "Already? Good grief, when did that happen?"

Denzel wrinkled his nose. "Just, you know, after the twentieth. It went sort of nineteenth, twentieth—"

Before Denzel could say more, her hand clamped across his mouth again. "Shh," she urged, her eyes darting back to the ceiling. "They're here."

Denzel looked up, but saw nothing. The only sounds he could hear were the howling winds and rattling rain, but something had spooked Mrs Gourlay. Considering that she *was* a literal spook, that didn't bode well.

"I need you to wait here for a wee while," she told him. "I'll go give our visitors a piece of my mind. If I don't come back... Well, if I don't come back, it was a pleasure to finally meet you."

She gave the necklace a prod. "Put that on. Keep it safe. And keep yourself safe too."

Denzel heard a sound from out in the hallway. It was the slow, metallic *shinkt* of a sword being drawn from a scabbard. A second followed, then a third. Denzel's pulse quickened. The Samurai-ghosts had found him.

Mrs Gourlay removed her hand, shot a sad look back to her skeleton, then smoothed down the front of her nightdress.

"Right, then," she said, and before Denzel could warn her what was waiting for her, she slipped past him and straight through the wall.

Her voice came from the other side, muffled by the decaying plaster. "Hasn't anyone ever taught you lassies to knock before entering?" she asked. "I'm afraid I'm going to have to ask you to—"

There was the sound of a sword *whumming* through the air, a faint "Ya!" from one of the Samurai-ghosts and then silence.

Denzel held his breath, the necklace making a little *chinking* sound as it trembled in his grip. They'd killed her. Or ... double-killed her. Or whatever it was that you did to ghosts. She'd tried to help him, and they'd double-killed her. And now he was trapped in here with them lurking just outside.

He had just started to quietly backtrack towards the window when Mrs Gourlay's voice came again. "Well now, that wasn't very nice, was it?"

Denzel could almost feel the Samurai-ghosts' confusion radiating through the wall. A sword *whummed* again, hacking and slashing a few times in quick succession.

There was silence again. Denzel glanced back to the window, convinced that they'd definitely double-killed her this time. Maybe even triple-killed her.

He was wrong.

"Och, now look what you've done," said Mrs Gourlay, sounding really quite annoyed. "Looks like I'm going to have to teach you lassies a lesson."

A sound followed. Denzel knew he'd never be able to describe what the sound was like if asked. At best, he'd be able to say it was the sound of something small becoming something much larger in quite a short space of time.

The floorboards *creaked* in protest. The wall ahead of him shook, sending cracks racing across the rotten plaster.

There was a short, sharp scream that ended very abruptly.

There was some frantic sword-slashing, followed

by a *splat*.

There was some high-pitched shouting in a language Denzel didn't understand. It became a gargle, then a wheeze, then a squelchy sort of farting noise that eventually faded into silence.

Denzel eyed the window again, considering whether he should make a run for it while he had the chance. Before he could come to a decision, though, the bedroom door flew open and the room was filled with a blazing white light.

Hissing and shielding his eyes, Denzel stepped back. He watched through his fingers as the blinding glow took the form of Mrs Gourlay.

Except, she wasn't Mrs Gourlay. Not really. She was much younger, her grey hair tumbling in long auburn locks down her back. Her frail, fragile body now looked supple and strong. Her skin was perfectly smooth, as if someone had carefully ironed out every crease.

Her eyes were no longer clouded. They shimmered in the light that seemed to be radiating from somewhere inside her. Where the light touched the structure of the house, it too was renewed. The rot and damp were pushed aside, restoring the paintwork and wallpaper. Denzel watched in wonder as the room repaired itself around him, and the threadbare carpet bloomed back to its original colour and thickness.

Mrs Gourlay floated into the room, hovering several centimetres above the floor. She trembled slightly, her hair blowing in a wind that Denzel couldn't feel or hear.

"All right?" Denzel asked her. It felt a bit understated, given the circumstances, but he knew he had to say something, and that was the best he'd been able to come up with.

"You're safe now, Denzel," Mrs Gourlay replied. Her voice was stronger, and yet somehow lighter, as if she was about to break into song. Denzel really hoped she wasn't. The situation was already weird enough. "For the moment, at least. But I fear great danger still awaits."

"Yeah, it usually does," Denzel said.

"Put the necklace on," Mrs Gourlay instructed, and Denzel thought it was probably best not to argue. He pulled it over his head and tucked the pendant inside his jacket.

He looked around the bedroom. It now looked immaculate, spoiled only by the skeleton propped up in the bed. Although, Denzel noted, even that looked as if it had been given a quick polish. "What happens now?"

"Now my work is done. I've finished the job," said Mrs Gourlay. "I can rest now."

Her face was a picture of joy, her eyes gazing at something behind. A sob caught in her throat. A tear rolled down her perfectly smooth cheek.

"It's *beautiful*," she whispered.

Denzel turned in the direction Mrs Gourlay was staring. He saw nothing but the curtains, and they weren't anything worth writing home about. Nothing to get emotional over, anyway.

It occurred to him that she might be seeing something that he wasn't. Either that or she *really* liked those curtains.

"Goodbye, Denzel," Mrs Gourlay said. She smiled at him, and he felt warmth tingle across his skin. "Goodbye and good luck."

The glow that was radiating from her became painfully bright, forcing Denzel to bury his face in his arms and screw his eyes tightly shut.

And then, as quickly as it had started, the glow faded. Denzel waited for a few moments before daring to open his eyes.

A single candle sat on the floor, casting its glow across the dirty, stained walls and worn carpet. The ghost of Mrs Gourlay was gone, and all her magical DIY home improvements had gone with her.

Denzel bent to retrieve the candle and crept out into

the hallway. Three gloopy green smears were splattered across the floor and walls. As Denzel watched, three Samurai swords became mist, then drifted away.

Suddenly a figure came lunging through the cottage's front door, making Denzel scream in fright. It stumbled towards him, eyes wide, hair standing on end, hands grabbing.

It took three seconds for Denzel's brain to process what he was seeing, and a further two for him to stop screaming.

The wild-looking ghostly figure beamed happily at him.

"Wow, it's windy out there," said Smithy, smoothing his hair down. He looked Denzel up and down, glanced briefly at the ectoplasm splodges, then puffed out his cheeks. "So then, what did I miss?"

CHAPTER 11

Denzel had too many questions of his own to launch straight into an explanation of what had happened to him.

"Where's everyone else? Are they OK? What happened to the hood guys?" he asked.

Smithy counted on his fingers. "Hood guys magicked away, everyone's OK ..."

The door was kicked open and Boyle charged in, blaster rifle raised. Samara entered behind him, hands raised and glowing with magical energy.

"... and here they are now," Smithy concluded.

A finger tapped Denzel on the shoulder, making him

scream in fright again. He turned to find Tabatha standing there, looking almost as dishevelled as Smithy.

"Sorry, didn't meant to frighten you," she said.

"I wasn't frightened," Denzel insisted.

"Then why did you scream?" Smithy asked.

"It wasn't a scream. It was a…" His mind raced for a moment, then he shrugged. "No, you're right, it was a scream. Fair enough."

He eyed Tabatha suspiciously. "So … she's *not* a bad guy?"

"No! It was just a trick," said Smithy. His face took on a vague, dream-like appearance as he stared at the other ghost. "Just a trick. Just a clever, cunning, beautiful trick."

Tabatha gave a little wave of her hand. "Aw, tweren't nothing," she said.

"Clear!" barked Boyle, lowering his weapon. The sudden shout snapped Smithy out of his daze.

"Uh, yeah. We noticed," said Smithy. "But thanks for double-checking. Good job."

Samara rushed to Denzel and began checking him over. She placed her thumbs on his cheeks and pulled down so she could get a better look at his eyes, then tilted his head back and looked up his nose.

"What are you doing?" Denzel asked.

"I'm checking you're you," Samara told him. She

pulled open his mouth and peered inside, then prodded his tongue. Something electrical sparked through it, snapping Denzel's mouth shut.

"Ow! What was that?"

"Spectral resonance test," Samara said. She licked her finger and stuck it in one of Denzel's ears. "Say 'Aah'."

"Cut that out!" Denzel protested. He tried to pull away, but Samara's finger squirmed deeper into his ear. "Fine. *Aah*. There. Happy now?"

Samara nodded and stepped back. "OK, good."

"One more thing," said Smithy. He lunged forward and twisted both of Denzel's nipples.

Denzel cried out and jumped clear. "Ow! What's that meant to test for?"

"Hmm? Oh, nothing," said Smithy with a smirk. "Just thought it'd be a laugh."

Boyle's boot *squelched* in a blob of the green goo. He scowled as he raised his foot, and the gloop stretched from the bottom like elastic.

"Ectoplasm," he said. "Where did this come from? What happened here?"

"Three of those ghosts with the swords," Denzel said.

"And you dephantomised them?" said Boyle, his eyes widening with surprise.

Denzel shot Samara a questioning look.

"He means did you turn them into goo?" she explained.

"Oh. No. Not me," Denzel said. He pointed through the door into the bedroom. Mrs Gourlay's skeleton grinned at them through the darkness. "Her."

Everyone peered into the room.

Then everyone looked at Denzel.

After a moment, Samara stuck a finger back in his ear again.

"Get off!" Denzel protested. "Not the skeleton! Her ghost. Her ghost was here. She took care of the sword ghosts. And she gave me something."

"Was it a big kiss?" asked Smithy.

"Ew! No!" Denzel replied. "Why would she...? Doesn't matter, forget I asked." He unzipped his jacket a little to reveal the pendant. "It was this."

Everyone stared at it for a while. Eventually, Tabatha gave a low whistle. "That is one ugly necklace."

"I quite like it," said Smithy. "It's understated."

Boyle grabbed the necklace and yanked Denzel closer as he examined the pendant.

"Just go ahead and help yourself," Denzel told him. "Don't mind me."

"What is it?" asked Samara.

"Give me a second," Boyle told her. He studied the skull carefully, clicking his tongue against the roof of his mouth as he turned it over a few times, checking it from every angle.

"Mrs Gourlay, the old woman, she said it should follow the Ghostfather," said Denzel.

"How can it follow the Ghostfather?" Samara wondered.

Denzel shrugged, which seemed to really irritate Boyle, who was still examining the necklace.

"Stay still!"

"She also showed me a vision," said Denzel, his skin itching at the memory of it. "Of the Ghostfather. It wasn't very nice."

"What happened in it?" Tabatha asked.

Denzel puffed out his cheeks. "Everyone died, basically. Whole world destroyed, oceans boiling, cities falling. That sort of thing."

"Ah. The usual then," said Samara.

Denzel smiled weakly, having grave second thoughts about being part of an organisation whose members referred to the end of the world as "the usual".

With a grunt, Boyle shook his head and looked up from the skull pendant. "It's nothing. It's just an ugly skull necklace."

"Let an expert have a crack at it," Samara said, stepping in and taking the pendant from him, forcing Denzel to shuffle around to his right.

"I could take it off, you know," he protested. "You just have to ask."

Samara angled the pendant towards the candlelight. She examined it in silence for a while, very occasionally giving a little "Mm-hmm" as if figuring out some new piece of information.

"No, you're right, it's nothing," she finally admitted.

Tabatha held out a hand. "May I? I'm pretty experienced when it comes to this sort of thing."

"I bet you're *brilliant* at this sort of thing," Smithy told her.

Samara shot Boyle an uncertain look. He gave a brief shake of his head, but Samara decided to ignore him, and passed the pendant to Tabatha.

"Seriously, I'll take it off," said Denzel, shuffling around again.

Tabatha glanced briefly at the necklace's thick chain, then brought the pendant closer to her nose and sniffed deeply. She thought for a moment, then had another sniff.

"What is she doing?" Boyle grunted.

He grimaced as Tabatha licked the skull's gold face, then flicked her tongue in and out a few times.

"You know that's been in a dead woman's drawer for,

like, a hundred years, right?" said Denzel, his nostrils flaring in disgust.

"This is a waste of time," Boyle said.

"It's Mesopotamian," Tabatha announced. "It was crafted in 3,500 BC." She gave it another lick. "On a Wednesday. Around teatime."

Boyle snorted. "Shut up! There's no way she can know that."

Tabatha grinned. "OK, I'm lying about the Wednesday teatime thing, but the date's not far off."

"Except that symbol isn't Mesopotamian," Samara pointed out. "There are no records of them using any similar designs."

"Well, they must have," Tabatha said. "The taste test never lies. Although..." She licked it again. "It's been somewhere else too. More recent."

"Is it Scotland?" Boyle sneered.

"I meant somewhere between Scotland and Ancient Mesopotamia," Tabatha replied. "Japan, I think."

"That would tie with the Samurai-ghosts," said Denzel.

"You're welcome," said Tabatha. She let go of the pendant, letting it fall back against Denzel's chest.

Smithy clapped his hands and nodded his approval. "Great detective work! Really impressive."

"It's not impressive," said Boyle. "She licked a necklace

and then said some stuff we can't possibly verify. How is that great detective work?"

Smithy leaned closer to Tabatha. "Don't listen to him. He's a Jealous Jenny."

"I'm a what?" Boyle demanded. He shot Samara a sideways look. "What did he call me?"

"I think he said you're jealous," Samara replied.

"Of what? Of her?" Boyle snapped. "Jealous of being able to lick a piece of old jewellery and make some stuff up?"

"Jealous Jenny, Jealous Jenny," Smithy sang.

Boyle dead-eyed him. "I will blast you," he warned. "I will blast you in the face with this ghost-gun."

"I think we should head back to base," Tabatha said. She gestured to the door with her cane. "There's no saying those cult guys won't come back."

"Good idea," Samara agreed.

"What? Why are we listening to her now?" Boyle demanded. "Since when was she part of the team? Who even is she?"

"Her name's Tabatha," Smithy explained. "She's a gho—"

"I know who she is!" Boyle snapped. "But why's she giving orders all of a sudden? She doesn't get to decide when we go back to base!"

Tabatha raised her hands in surrender. "He's right. I've overstepped the mark. It's not my call to make," she said. She raised her eyebrows and smiled innocently at Boyle. "What do you suggest we do?"

All eyes went to Boyle. He shifted uncomfortably in the puddle of goo, then gave a sigh. "I think we should go back to base," he muttered.

Tabatha spun her cane and tucked it under her arm. "Good call," she said, then she motioned to Samara with a flourish. "Shall we?"

Boyle muttered darkly below his breath. Samara found herself fighting back a smile. Her fingers weaved a pattern in the air and light trails sparkled around them.

"Great, this again," Denzel groaned.

"Oh, quit complaining," Samara told him. "You'll barely even notice you're moving."

The last couple of words of the sentence were drowned out by the sound of Denzel's head collapsing into his chest and his feet becoming long, stringy tendrils of meat and gristle. His eyes inflated inside his shrinking skull. His arms folded inwards and outwards at the same time, as all his internal organs began an elaborate dance around the twisting labyrinth of his insides.

The universe became a kaleidoscope of colours, shapes, and even concepts that he couldn't put words to.

The cottage's walls tumbled away. The ceiling imploded. The floor made its excuses and left quietly through the back door.

And then, with a jolt that rattled his teeth in their sockets, Denzel was deposited in a mostly featureless white room back at Spectre Collectors Headquarters. The others appeared around him one by one, with Samara arriving last of all.

There was a loud ringing in his ears that was giving him a headache. It screamed at him from every direction at once, drilling into his skull almost like an—

"Alarm!" barked Boyle, bringing up his blaster rifle and spinning towards the room's only door. "That's the alarm."

"What does that mean?" asked Denzel. He tried to stand up, but his legs hadn't fully recovered from the magical transportation, and he just sort of flopped on the floor like a fish.

"It means we're in trouble," said Samara. She flicked her wrists and two balls of flame appeared around her hands. "Spectre Collectors HQ is under attack!"

CHAPTER 12

"Under attack?! We can't be under attack!" Denzel yelped. "How can we be under attack?!"

As if in answer to his question, the door to the room exploded off its hinges and slammed against the opposite wall. Something bear-sized and slimy stumbled in, a multitude of eyes blazing angrily. Six differently shaped hands balled into fists when the thing saw them.

"What the heck is that thing?" Denzel yelped.

"It's OK, I've got this," said Smithy, stepping forward. "Question One. Are you a good ghost?"

The thing roared at him. Its whole face opened as if on hinges, revealing hundreds of tiny, gnashing mouths.

Smithy stepped back again. "I'm going to take that as a no," he said.

Boyle pumped several energy rounds into the thing's chest. They didn't seem to do much damage to it, but they did force it back out of the room.

Samara stepped past him, her hands weaving a complex pattern in the air. There was a *whumpf* as the monster was compacted into a tiny cube. Almost immediately, the walls of the box began to buckle and bulge.

"Can't hold it," Samara warned, her hands shaking. "It's too strong."

Tabatha slipped past her, swinging her cane like a baseball bat. It hit the cube with a *crack*, launching it across the corridor. It slipped through the opposite wall like a ghost and, presumably, kept going.

"That should buy us some time," Tabatha said.

"Brilliant!" said Smithy, grinning goofily at her. "You saved us."

"I shot it!" Boyle pointed out.

"Joint effort," Tabatha said.

Denzel poked his head out of the room. From both directions along the corridor he heard what he could only describe as "a racket". It was a mix of blaster fire, roaring, wailing, magical explosions, and just a suggestion of screaming. Add in the wailing of the alarm, and Denzel reckoned he was going to have a migraine for the rest of his life.

Of course, quite how long that life would be was another matter entirely.

"Scanning for paranormal energy," Boyle announced, taking a handheld device from his belt. It *bleeped* a few times, then let out a continuous high-pitched tone.

A moment later, it exploded.

"I'm guessing that's not good," Denzel squeaked.

"Considering I hadn't even turned it on, no," said Boyle. "Not good."

"Containment has been breached. The Spectral Storage Vaults have been emptied," Samara announced. Her eyes were white and glowing faintly, her hair squirming around on her head like snakes. "They're everywhere."

"What do we do?" Denzel asked.

"They must be here for you," Samara realised. "We need to get you out of here."

Denzel felt like he should probably put up some sort of protest. He was technically a Spectre Collector, after all. He should offer to stay and help.

From along the corridor, a monstrous roar was followed by several frantic cries for help.

"OK, sounds like a plan," said Denzel. "I mean, if they're looking for me and I'm not here, they might leave. Right? In a way, I'll actually be helping."

"My hero," said Boyle. He was tucked in against the door frame, his weapon raised, and was itching to join the battle. "Now, hurry up and magic him out of here while we still have a building left."

"Smithy, Tabatha, stay with him," Samara urged, her fingertips dancing.

"I can help here," said Tabatha.

"Help him," Samara replied. "Keep him safe."

Tabatha looked to the door for a moment, then back to Samara. Finally, she nodded. "Deal. Do your thing."

"Hold on. This might get bumpy," said Samara.

Denzel's eyes widened. "Surely not bumpier than last time!"

"Guess you'll find out," said Samara. She thrust her hands forward.

Denzel braced himself.

"Nng," he said, screwing his eyes shut.

He clenched his fists by his side.

"Mnk," he said, gritting his teeth.

After a few moments of this, he opened one eye. They were still in the same room, still being assaulted by the same din.

"That wasn't bumpy at all," said Smithy. "I didn't even feel us move."

"You didn't move," said Samara. She studied her fingertips for a moment, then thrust them out again. A few disappointing sparks spat from the ends and tumbled to the floor where they died away. "They're blocking transport spells. I can't magic you out. They don't want you getting away."

Something exploded elsewhere in the complex. The echoing *bang* was followed by a series of ghostly moans and whistling *whoooos* that made Denzel want to run and hide under the covers of the closest available bed.

"What do we do?" Smithy asked.

Denzel swallowed and pulled himself up to his full height. It wasn't nearly as impressive as he'd hoped. "I guess I help fight."

Boyle snorted. "Good one. We can send you in one of the escape pods," he said. He twisted a dial on his rifle and something that looked a bit like a watch was ejected from the side. He tossed it to Denzel, who didn't react fast enough.

"Ow, careful!" Denzel protested, rubbing his forehead where the device had hit him. He bent to pick it up, then turned it over in his hands. "What's this?"

"Security key. It'll activate the pods and let you set

your destination."

Denzel slipped the device over his wrist. It immediately shrank to fit. "And what is our destination?" he wondered.

Another explosion rocked the complex. More ghostly moans came echoing along the corridor.

"Anywhere but here," Samara suggested. "You ready?"

Denzel nodded. "Ready."

"Smithy?"

Smithy blinked. "Hmm?"

"Are you ready?"

"For what?" asked Smithy. "I wasn't really listening."

Tabatha clamped a hand on his shoulder. Smithy gave a contended little sigh. "He's ready," Tabatha said. "Let's do it."

Denzel raced along a raised walkway, ducking low with his hands over his head as laser fire, bolts of magic and ghostly ectoplasmic blasts screamed past above and below him.

"Oh god, oh god, oh god," he whispered, scampering as quickly as he could towards the staircase at the other end of the narrow platform.

He was high above one of the underground complex's grand halls, trying very hard not to look down to the floor far below. This hall was the only one in the building big enough to hold all the Spectre Collectors at once, and was usually reserved for parades or big events.

There was definitely a "big event" taking place in it today, although not one it had ever been intended to hold.

The whole placed heaved with Vulterons in body armour, and Oberons with enchanted shields. They fired weapons and launched fireballs at a vast boiling cloud of Spectral Energy that thrashed in the air above them. Every few seconds, a shapeless apparition would break from the heaving mass and swoop in to attack the Spectre Collectors below, leading to more panicky firing and several outbursts of angry shouting.

The walkway that Denzel and the others were running across was so high that they were above the ghost cloud. For the moment, none of the spooks seemed to have noticed his presence, but if his usual luck was anything to go by, it would just be a matter of time.

Sure enough, just as Denzel reached the top of the staircase, something white and vaporous came flying up the top few steps. He felt a blast of arctic coldness as the thing passed through him, and then his lungs cramped up and his muscles went tight.

He tried to turn, but his limbs were no longer obeying instructions; tried to speak, but his mouth was no longer under his control.

Samara placed a hand on his back. "Vacate," she hissed, and Denzel saw the ghost go shooting out from inside his chest. He sagged to the floor just as Boyle shot the spirit with an energy bolt, turning it into a blob of spectral slime.

"Thanks," Denzel wheezed.

"You're welcome," said Samara. She gestured to the stairs. "You three go. Get to the escape pods and get out. We'll find you."

"What will you do?" said Denzel. "You should come with us."

Samara shook her head. "We have to stay here and help."

She joined Boyle by the railing and peered down into the spectral cloud. Their eyes met for a moment, and then they nodded.

"See you down there," Boyle said. He vaulted over the railing and fell, roaring and firing, into the ghostly fog.

Samara stepped up on to the railing, muttered a quiet incantation, then fell forwards like a diver from the top board. Her hands radiated magical energy as she was swallowed by the thrashing mass.

"OK, even I have to admit that was pretty cool," said

Tabatha. She caught Denzel by the wrist and dragged him down the stairs. "Now, come on, Chosen One. We're getting you out of here."

CHAPTER 13

Denzel and Smithy skidded around a corner into a corridor swarming with ghosts, monsters and other general unpleasantness.

They got a brief glimpse of two Spectre Collectors – one Oberon, one Vulteron – standing back to back in the centre of the horde before Tabatha caught them both and pulled them into cover.

"OK, not that way," she said, turning and searching for another exit. The room they were in was a smaller hall attached to the main one. Spectral Energy was seeping through the wall and oozing down it like a thick green sweat.

SPECTRE COLLECTORS

"Cor, this is exciting, isn't it?" Smithy whispered. "Here, Denzel, what would you rather, right?"

"Not now, Smithy!" Denzel hissed. He peeked around the corner into the corridor they'd almost run down and realised with a start that the Spectre Collectors currently surrounded by scary things were Knightley and Rasmus.

They were vastly outnumbered, and from the way Knightley was swinging with her fists, it looked like she was out of ammo.

Denzel groaned. "We have to help them," he said.

"No, we have to get you out of here," Tabatha replied. "They're all here looking for you. We can't let them get you." She gestured ahead to another corridor that looked to be ghost-free. "Come on, this way."

Her hand clamped around Denzel's wrist again, tightening like a handcuff. With a tug, she pulled him away from the corridor, leaving Knightley and Rasmus to whatever grisly fate awaited them.

They'd never liked Denzel.

Denzel had never liked them.

He sighed. Still, he couldn't just leave them.

"Hey! Chosen One right here!" he hollered.

Along the corridor, a multitude of misshapen heads turned at the sound of his voice. A legion of horrifying faces twisted in rage.

"OK, so that was a mistake," Denzel whimpered.

"Run!" Tabatha cried, pushing Denzel ahead. She twirled her cane and opened fire with a volley of blasts as the monsters came lumbering after them.

"We can get to the escape pods this way," Smithy said, grabbing Denzel and plunging into the mouth of another corridor.

"How do you know that?" Denzel wheezed.

"I can sense it," said Smithy. He pointed to the wall. "And there's a big sign there that says 'Escape Pods' on it. That also helped."

Tabatha caught up with them a moment later. She shoved them both on, forcing them to run faster.

"Did you get them?" Smithy asked, shooting her a look back over his shoulder.

"Yes," she said. There was a chorus of roaring from somewhere behind her. "If by 'getting them' you mean making them much, *much* angrier."

"There!" cried Denzel, spotting a door marked "Escape Pods". Tabatha paused to fire a couple of blasts backwards along the corridor, then followed the boys.

Denzel gulped down a quick breath before Smithy pulled him through the door. They stumbled into a brightly lit room with a dozen telephone-box-sized metal boxes spaced evenly around it.

"Go, go!" Tabatha urged, spinning to watch the door.

"Which one?" Denzel asked. "Does it matter?"

"Any one!" Tabatha yelped. A skull-like head appeared through the door. She *thwacked* it with her cane, driving it back. "Just hurry!"

Smithy stopped between two of the boxes. "Eenie, Meenie, Miney..."

"This one!" Denzel decided, pulling open the door and jumping inside. The space inside was a tight fit for him and Smithy, and even more so when Tabatha squeezed in beside them. She and Smithy found themselves face to face. Smithy's pale skin blushed bright red. He tried to smile, but it turned into a weird sort of grimace instead.

"H-hi there," Smithy stammered. "I'm Smithy."

Denzel groaned. "Oh, good grief. She knows your name, Smithy."

Smithy sighed happily. "She knows my name!"

The door slammed shut. A locking mechanism went *clunk*. From outside there came the unmistakable *kaaraack* of a door being smashed down.

"How does it work?" asked Denzel, frantically searching for some sort of launch button. "How do we make it—"

The bracelet Boyle had given him buzzed on his wrist. Denzel screamed as the pod rocketed upwards. It was only the fact that he was squashed between Smithy and

Tabatha that stopped him being slammed against the floor as the escape pod screamed up through a tube in the ceiling.

As it rose, the metal of the pod became semi-transparent, affording Denzel an all-too-clear view of the smooth tube walls that hurtled past just centimetres away on either side of them. The ceiling was see-through too, and Denzel found himself becoming increasingly concerned about the dead end that seemed to be looming ahead of them in the half-darkness.

He screamed again. It seemed like the only sensible solution.

"We're going to crash!"

Just before they did, the barrier opened, as if on a hinge. The pod rocketed out of the darkness and into bright sunshine. Denzel caught a glimpse of a headstone and an open grave, then of a graveyard and the church building built on top of the Spectre Collectors' underground headquarters.

The pod climbed quickly, and in moments the church and other buildings around it looked like toys. Denzel closed his eyes, fighting back a panic attack.

When he opened them again, the whole town was spread out below him like a map. And they were still climbing.

"Where are we escaping to?" he whispered. "Space?"

"Whoa! That would be cool!" said Smithy. "I've always wanted to go to space!"

"I haven't!" Denzel squeaked. Beads of moisture formed on the outside of the pod, and Denzel realised they must be passing through a cloud.

"Nah, nor me, until about five seconds ago," Smithy admitted. "Still, exciting though. You think there'll be aliens? I bet there'll be aliens."

Before anyone could respond, a soothing female voice chimed from a hidden speaker. "Escape velocity achieved. Please select destination."

"Space!" said Smithy.

Denzel elbowed him.

"No, not space!" he said. "Down. Take us down!"

"Destination confirmed," said the voice of the pod.

They stopped abruptly, lifting Denzel off his feet and slamming him into the ceiling. He'd barely had time to register this before the pod began to fall. The air whistled around the pod as it plunged towards the ground below. Still pressed against the ceiling, Denzel came to the conclusion that "down" may not have been the best instruction to give.

"Change destination," Tabatha said. She and Smithy had braced themselves against the sides of the box so they didn't go flying upwards like Denzel had done. Unlike Denzel, there was a very good chance the ceiling wouldn't have stopped them.

The pod continued to drop, the whistling increasing as it picked up speed. From up on the ceiling, Denzel saw the world growing steadily larger.

"Alter destination. Change course. Amend route," Tabatha instructed, her voice becoming a touch more hysterical each time. The pod ignored her.

"I'm not a Spectre Collector," she concluded. "One of you needs to do it."

"Stop!" said Smithy.

The pod stopped in mid-air. Denzel barely had time to eject a terrified snort before he was hammered against the floor. The sudden halt temporarily turned Smithy incorporeal. He passed straight through the floor, continued downwards for thirty or forty metres, then drifted back up into the pod.

"Yikes. That was close," he said.

Down at his feet, Denzel groaned and slowly untangled himself. "Speak for yourself," he wheezed, wincing in pain as he clicked his various limbs and fingers back into place.

A hundred tiny agonies zapped through him as he pulled himself to his feet. The escape pod was hanging in mid-air a few thousand metres above the ground, a faint blue light pulsing beneath it.

"What now?" Denzel whispered.

Tabatha peered down through the floor. "We can't just go back down there. They wanted me to get you out of danger."

"I don't feel very out of danger," Denzel said. "I feel very *in* danger, actually."

Smithy frowned. "Why?"

"Because we're hovering thousands of metres up in the air in a glass box!" Denzel pointed out.

Smithy looked down. "Oh. Yeah. Forgot about that. Wait, aren't you scared of heights?"

"Yes!"

"Like, *really terrified*?"

"Yes!"

Smithy nodded. "Thought so. Then we should probably get dow—"

Tabatha clamped a hand over his mouth, which immediately became the greatest thing that had ever happened to him.

"Don't say 'down'," she warned.

Smithy looked confused for a moment, then nodded to indicate his understanding. Tabatha removed her hand from his mouth.

"So if we're not going *in that direction*," said Smithy, pointing to the floor, "then where are we going?"

Tabatha clicked her tongue against the back of her teeth. "I have an idea. But it's a bit off the wall," she said. She flashed Denzel an apologetic smile. "And you're probably going to wish you'd gone to the toilet before we left."

Denzel looked confused. "Huh? Why? Where are we going?"

"East," said Tabatha. "*Far* east..."

CHAPTER 14

Denzel hopped out of the pod and ran as fast he could towards a clump of bushes, hurriedly fiddling with the button of his trousers.

Tabatha and Smithy stepped out after him, and made a point of ignoring the sigh of relief that rose from behind the bushes a moment later.

Night was drawing in fast, and the sky was a palette of pinks and purples. Tabatha looked up, marvelling at it in silence.

Smithy danced awkwardly on the spot, watching Tabatha. She had already switched from admiring the evening sky to taking in their surroundings, checking for signs of trouble. The only danger at the moment was a slight risk of flooding from Denzel.

It really had been a long trip.

A moment later, Denzel emerged from behind the bush. He looked quite a lot more relaxed than he had done for the past hour and a half.

"Feeling better now?" Smithy asked. "All done in the toilet department?"

"Much better," said Denzel slightly sheepishly.

While the boys talked, Tabatha climbed up to the top of the escape pod and balanced on it. She turned in slow, steady circles, her eyes scanning the scenery around them.

Bushes and cherry blossom trees stood on one side. On the other, a large mirror-like lake stretched across to a snow-capped mountain in the distance. The pinks and purples of the evening sky were perfectly reflected in the smooth water.

Smithy put his hands on his hips and joined her in looking around. "So," he said, nodding sagely. "This is France."

"Japan," Tabatha corrected.

Smithy raised his eyebrows. "Huh?"

"It's Japan."

Smithy stared blankly up at her.

"Not France," Denzel clarified.

"Did we get lost?" Smithy asked.

"No. We're not lost," said Tabatha. "We were supposed to come to Japan."

"Were we?" asked Smithy, looking highly doubtful. "Why would we do that?"

Tabatha pointed to the pendant around Denzel's neck. "Because that was in Japan before it was in Scotland," she said.

"And because of the Samurai-ghosts," added Denzel. "They're our best lead. We had a whole conversation about all this in the escape pod."

Smithy nodded. "Aha! Is that when you were both talking a lot and I played noughts and crosses on the window?"

"Yes. That was then," Denzel confirmed.

"Gotcha," said Smithy. "Oh, and I won, by the way. In case you were wondering. And yet at the same time, I lost. It was a real roller coaster."

He looked around. "There doesn't seem to be a lot here. Nice mountain though. They call that one Mont Blanc."

"Mount Fuji," Tabatha corrected. "Mont Blanc is in France."

"Right. Right," said Smithy. He pointed to the ground

at his feet. "And this is…?"

Tabatha jumped down from the top of the pod and landed between Denzel and Smithy. "Japan. But I don't get it. The pod was supposed to take us to the local Spectre Collectors base. There's nothing here."

"Or *is* there?" said Smithy in a mysterious whisper.

Denzel and Tabatha both looked at him. "Is there?" Denzel asked.

"I don't know," said Smithy. "That's what I was asking you. Is there? I have no idea."

Denzel tutted, then crossed to the pod. He leaned in through the open door, being careful not to step inside in case the thing suddenly took off again.

"Um, hi," he said. "You said you'd take us to the Japanese Spectre Collectors HQ."

"Affirmative," came the reply. "We have arrived at the entrance."

Denzel turned and regarded the scenery around them. "Is it in the bushes?" he wondered.

"Negative," the voice chimed. "Would you like me to activate the entryway?"

Denzel checked with Tabatha, who nodded her approval. "Go for it."

"Uh, OK. Yeah. Sure," said Denzel, turning his attention back to the inside of the pod. "Activate it."

"Confirmed," said the pod. "Entrance activating in three, two—"

Denzel didn't get to hear the "one". Instead, a swirling vortex of pearlescent blue light opened behind him, and a sudden gale knocked him off his feet. He caught a fleeting glimpse of Tabatha and Smithy both tumbling through the air beside him, and then the world turned icy cold around him as he was swallowed by the light.

Denzel was the first to be ejected through the other side of the entrance. He flapped and flailed as he tumbled through the air, then he bounced into a net, rolled clumsily backwards, and landed in an undignified heap on the floor.

A moment later Smithy shot by above him, passed through the net and became solid just in time to *thud* against the wall behind it. While he slid slowly down it, Tabatha hopped through the portal and alighted stealthily, her cane raised and at the ready.

The entranceway snapped shut, revealing what looked like some sort of security checkpoint. It reminded Denzel of the immigration desk he and Smithy had to go through at the airport in New York.

A little booth stood directly ahead of them next to a revolving metal gate. The bottom half of the booth was made of a dark, polished wood with various Japanese letters carved into it. The top half was glass, with no visible openings that Denzel could spot. A little speaker was mounted on the shelf where the wood met the glass, presumably so someone outside could hear whoever was inside.

There was nobody inside now, though, unless they were very short. There was nobody else in the room, in fact, and although there was nothing obviously wrong, something tingled uneasily across Denzel's scalp.

Through the gate was a sliding door made up of lots of white panels. From this distance, they looked like paper, although Denzel was fairly certain they'd be something more secure than that.

Mind you...

He turned slowly on the spot, taking in the rest of the room. There was no door behind him, just a painting of the same mountain scene they'd arrived at in the escape pod. The only way in and out of the room was either through the sliding door, or the magic one they'd come through. He supposed that, as secure entrances went, "only accessible via a mystical portal" was up there with the best of them.

"It's smaller than I expected," said Smithy.

"I doubt this is the whole thing," said Denzel. He

pointed to the door. "I think everything else is probably that way."

"Uh, guys," said Tabatha. She was over by the security booth, peering in through the glass at something on the floor. "You'd better see this."

Denzel and Smithy exchanged worried looks, then joined her at the booth. Denzel immediately let out a gasp. The window was quite high, so Smithy had to stretch up on his tiptoes to see the floor on the other side.

When that didn't prove enough, he levitated a few centimetres until he was high enough to see over the shelf to the floor below.

"What am I looking for?" Smithy asked.

Denzel shot him a sideways look, then nodded in the direction of the floor. "Him!"

"The man?" asked Smithy.

"Yes, the man! Of course the man!" Denzel replied.

There was a man lying on the floor. Well, technically a teenager, Denzel thought, but close enough. He wore a variation of a Vulteron uniform that looked like something that would be reserved for parades. The camouflage and colours were the same, but it was all shiny buttons and neat lines, and nothing like the combat fatigues Boyle wore.

For a moment, Denzel wondered if Boyle, Samara and the others were OK, but then he returned to the more pressing matter of the man on the floor.

"Is he dead?" Smithy asked, his voice dropping to a whisper as if he was scared of offending the motionless figure.

"I don't know," Denzel replied. "Phase through and check."

"*You* phase through and check!" said Smithy.

"I can't," Denzel pointed out.

"Well, I'm not touching him!" Smithy retorted. "He might be dead! Or worse, he might be alive, and when I go to touch him he might jump up and go 'Wargh!' at me." He shook his head emphatically. "No. There's no way I'm going in there. Not in a million years."

Tabatha raised an eyebrow. "Scared?"

"Fine, I'll do it," said Smithy, immediately phasing into the booth. He looked down at the figure on the floor, but kept out of grabbing distance. "Hello?" he said. "Are you dead?"

"He's hardly going to say 'yes', is he?" Denzel pointed out.

"He might," said Smithy. "I would."

"Check properly," Denzel urged.

"Properly. Right," said Smithy. He took a moment to

steady himself, then put a foot on the man's chest and jiggled him a bit.

That done, he immediately jumped backwards, shut his eyes and started flailing wildly with his fists.

After a few moments of this, he opened his eyes and stopped swinging. The man hadn't moved a muscle.

Smithy lowered his hands. "Definitely dead," he confirmed, then he was brushed aside when Tabatha phased into the booth beside him.

Squatting beside the fallen figure, she placed a finger on his throat and checked for a pulse. "He's not dead," she announced.

"I'm pretty sure he is," said Smithy. "I've seen alive people before, and they're usually moving."

Tabatha dug her fingers up under the man's jaw and then, to Smithy's horror, pulled his face off.

"Well, he's bound to be dead now," he remarked, then he got a clear view of the man's skull. It was made of a clear plastic, with dozens of little motors built into the structure.

"See? Not dead. Just a robot," said Tabatha. She looked down at the plastic skull again and nodded appreciatively. "It's pretty cool actually."

Being the only person in the group not able to walk through solid walls, Denzel had taken it upon himself to creep over to the door. Up close, the white panels did seem to be made of paper, and the door was light enough to easily slide aside a few centimetres, allowing Denzel to see into the room beyond.

He stared for a moment, then quietly slid the door closed.

"Um, we've got a problem," he said, turning to face the booth. Tabatha and Smithy both emerged through the side.

"Is it your hair?" asked Smithy. "I know. I didn't want to say anything."

"No, it's— Wait, what's wrong with my hair?" Denzel asked, reaching up and giving it a pat. He quickly came to the conclusion that now wasn't the time to concern himself with it.

Jabbing a thumb over his shoulder, Denzel dropped his voice to a whisper. "I think there's been..."

His voice tailed off. He gave a shake of his head. "In fact, it's probably best if you see it for yourself."

CHAPTER 15

Taking a deep breath, Denzel pulled the door aside. When he did, a scene of absolute chaos was revealed.

The room beyond was a large hangar full of what had presumably once been Vulteron equipment, but was now mostly smouldering piles of scrap. A Spook Suit – a towering suit of robot battle armour – lay in pieces on the floor, its components sparking and fizzing.

Several long racks of shelves were buckled and twisted, their contents lying broken and scattered all across the room. One of the room's fluorescent strip lights hung down, its broken cable sparking at the exposed end. The other lights flickered erratically, plunging the room into stuttering fits of darkness.

On the wall directly across from where Denzel and the others stood, someone had spray-painted a now all-too-familiar symbol.

"Well, I guess we know who did all this," Tabatha said.

Smithy nodded sagely. "Raccoons."

Tabatha turned to look at him. At this point in their relationship, Denzel didn't bother.

"Very destructive things, raccoons," said Smithy. "In America, they call them trash pandas."

"The Cult of Shantankar," said Tabatha. She pointed with her cane. "That's the symbol for the Ghostfather."

"Oh. Right. Gotcha," said Smithy. He regarded the symbol painted on the wall. "I did wonder how raccoons could get high enough to paint that, but thought if they made a sort of pyramid—"

"Shh," said Tabatha.

Smithy glanced around. "Why?"

"No reason. Just *shh*."

While they'd been talking, Denzel's eyes had fallen on one of the pieces of equipment that had been knocked on to the floor. It was a Spectral Energy Scanner, similar to the one Boyle used.

Picking the gadget up, Denzel turned it over in his hands, searching for the on switch. Boyle had let him play with one of the devices soon after he'd first joined the Spectre Collectors. Although, naturally, Boyle hadn't used the words "play with" because he had no concept of fun.

After a few moments of searching, Denzel found a slide switch and pushed it up. The scanner display lit up in oranges and reds. Several bar charts appeared at the bottom and began to fluctuate up and down.

"Finding anything?" Tabatha asked.

Denzel turned to her and Smithy and one of the lines on the display shot up to the top. He angled the gadget away and it dropped to around the halfway point.

"Found you two," he said.

"Well, that's not exactly fair," said Smithy. "You didn't give us time to hide."

"Getting anything that isn't us?" Tabatha asked.

Denzel consulted the scanner again, and took a few tentative steps further into the hangar. The display stayed mostly static, but for a moment he thought he saw a blip appear on the top part of the screen, which contained the long-range sensors. If there was something there, though, it didn't hang around long enough for Denzel to analyse it.

"Doesn't look like it," he said. "Seems pretty clear."

"Does it have a mode to scan for crazy cult people in

big robes?" Smithy asked.

"Sadly not," said Denzel. He kept the scanner running, but clipped it to his belt out of the way.

"OK, so here's what we need to start figuring out," Tabatha announced. She tucked her cane under one arm, then began counting on the fingers of her other hand. "One, what happened? Two, where is everyone? Three, is whoever did this still here?"

"Four, is that guy in the booth alive or dead?" Smithy asked.

"He's still a robot," said Tabatha.

"An alive robot or a dead robot?" Smithy wondered.

"A broken robot," said Tabatha. She raised another finger, then hesitated. "Great, now I've lost my train of thought."

She shrugged. "Let's focus on those first few and try to figure out what went down."

"How are we meant to do that?" Denzel asked.

"By exploring," said Tabatha. She whipped the cane out from beneath her arm and pointed ahead. "Onward!"

The hangar wasn't the only room to have suffered damage. A roll-up garage-style door had taken them into a corridor whose paintwork was an irregular pattern of cracks and scorch marks.

That, in turn, had led them to one of the more disturbing finds – an empty Spectral Storage Vault. Hundreds of drawers had been prised open, and all the gemstones containing ghosts removed from inside.

A few gems lay smashed on the floor, suggesting whoever had cleared the place out hadn't been very careful.

There were six other Spectral Storage Vaults on the same level as the first one. Tabatha phased through the walls of each of them, returning to confirm that they had all been cleared out in exactly the same way as the first.

The three of them continued along the curved corridor, stopping to check in every room they came across. They found no one. Offices stood empty. Briefing rooms were abandoned. The lights were on all over the complex, but it seemed like no one was home.

It was only when they'd been walking for a while that something occurred to Denzel. Something had been niggling away at him for a while, but he hadn't quite been able to put his finger on it until now.

"So, I've been thinking," he began.

"Was it about bees?" asked Smithy. "Because if so, me too."

"Uh, no. Not about bees," said Denzel.

Smithy looked disappointed. "Oh."

"Samara and Boyle said we should get me somewhere safe, right? Somewhere out of harm's way, away from the mad cult people."

"They did say that, yes," Tabatha confirmed. She had taken the lead and was striding along the corridor, her cane twirling like a marching band baton.

"Right," said Denzel. "It's just ... we don't seem to have done that. If anything, we seem to have gone looking for trouble. We came to Japan because we guessed that's where the Samurai-ghosts came from."

"Your point being?" asked Tabatha.

"It doesn't feel very safe," Denzel replied. "Like, if I'm trying to avoid something dangerous, I probably shouldn't actively go looking for that thing. Does that make sense?"

"Complete sense," Tabatha said. "If you were scared a lion was going to eat you, you wouldn't run into the lion cage at the zoo covered in gravy."

"Right! Right, exactly," said Denzel.

He looked pointedly at the scorched and damaged walls. "But it kind of feels like that's what we've done."

Tabatha stopped and turned to him. "OK, I suppose I should tell you."

"Tell me what?" Denzel asked.

"The truth. I probably should've told you a while ago, but better late than never, right?"

"Right," Denzel agreed. "I think." He frowned. "What are we talking about?"

"I didn't get captured by accident," Tabatha said. "By the Spectre Collectors, I mean. I got caught on purpose."

"Why?" asked Denzel.

Tabatha smiled. "So I could meet you."

"Him? Or me?" asked Smithy, leaning in.

"Him," said Tabatha. Smithy's shoulders slumped. "But you were a nice surprise," Tabatha added, and Smithy immediately perked up again.

"Why did you want to meet me?" Denzel asked.

"I'd heard rumours. Whispers about the end of the world, Chosen One, blah, blah, blah. The usual," Tabatha said. "I figured I couldn't leave you Spectre Collectors to have all the fun, so I got myself caught."

She leaned in closer, as if sharing some big secret. "See, stopping the end of the world is kind of my thing."

"I thought that was just on Tuesdays?" said Smithy.

"It is Tuesday," Tabatha said.

Denzel shook his head. "It's Monday."

"Time difference," Tabatha explained. "It's Tuesday here."

"Oh," said Denzel.

He took a moment to process everything that Tabatha had said.

"So … you're saying you've deliberately dragged me into danger?"

"Exactly!" said Tabatha, beaming proudly. She prodded him on the chest with her cane. "Here's the thing, Denzel. I've seen enough of these weird cult, 'We need the Chosen One'-type deals to know that you can't hide from it. They'll just keep coming and coming until they eventually get you. And then, once they've got you, they'll do horrible things to you."

"Like what?" asked Smithy.

"You don't want to know," said Tabatha.

Smithy considered this. "I'm pretty sure I do."

Denzel nodded slowly. "Which brings me back to my original point. Shouldn't we be getting as far away from them as possible?"

"Like I said, they'll find you sooner or later. They'll expect you to run. They won't expect you to attack them." Tabatha grinned. "We'll have the element of surprise. All we have to do is track down the cult, stop them unleashing the Ghostfather and save the world."

Denzel wasn't sure the element of surprise was enough of an advantage for them to accomplish all that, but before he could say as much, Tabatha's eyes were drawn to the Spectral Energy Scanner on his belt.

"Wait, what was that?" she asked, grabbing the device and unhooking it. "There!"

A single red blip flashed on the long-range scanner. "We're not alone," said Tabatha, her voice dropping into a low whisper. "There's another ghost in here with us."

CHAPTER 16

Tabatha studied the scanner, and the *blip* flashing on its screen. Smithy and Denzel drew closer together, their eyes darting around the corridor.

"What kind of ghost is it?" Smithy whispered. "Is it a mean one?"

"I don't know," said Tabatha.

"Is it a *big* ghost?" Smithy asked.

Tabatha held up the scanner for them to see. "Again, I don't know. It's a flashing red dot."

Smithy gave a little squeak of fear. "That's the worst kind of ghost of all!"

Denzel shot him a sideways look. "No, the ghost isn't a

flashing red dot. Just the reading on the scanner."

"Phew!" said Smithy, visibly relaxing. "That's fine then. You had me worried for a minute."

Tabatha handed Denzel the scanner, then turned silently on her heel and held her cane as if it were a rifle. "Lead the way," she urged. "Let's find out what we're dealing with."

Denzel wasn't keen on leading the way, but he did it anyway. The blip on the scanner moved gradually down towards the bottom of the screen as he shuffled along the corridor.

There was a set of double doors ahead and on the right. Judging by the rate at which the blip was moving down the screen, and the distance to the door, Denzel worked out that the ghost must be somewhere in the room beyond.

He pointed to the doors and they all crept closer, Tabatha drawing level with him so they were now walking side by side. Smithy, not wanting to be at the back on his own, squeezed into the gap between them.

"This is cosy, innit?" he whispered, only to be shushed by both of them.

There was a little plastic plaque on the door with some Japanese writing on it. Denzel had no idea what it said, and fired a hopeful look in Tabatha's direction.

"Can you translate that?"

"Yeah," she replied.

"Great!" said Denzel.

"If you give me forty minutes and a Japanese-to-English dictionary."

"Oh," said Denzel a little less enthusiastically.

"Vulteron Vehicle Storage," said Smithy.

Denzel and Tabatha both turned their heads and looked down at him. "What?" Denzel asked.

Smithy nodded to the sign. "Vulteron Vehicle Storage," he said. "Or maybe Vulteron Garage. You could read it either way."

"You speak Japanese?" Denzel gasped.

"What? No! Of course not!" Smithy laughed. He gave another nod to the sign. "I only read and write it."

"How? When? Why?" asked Denzel. "You've never mentioned it before."

"Why would I?" Smithy asked. "I've never mentioned a lot of things before. I can yodel too. I've never mentioned that before either."

To prove this, he drew in a breath and launched into some genuinely impressive yodelling, which was only cut short by Tabatha clamping a hand over his mouth. "Great. Well done. Now, shut up. Ghost through there, remember?"

Denzel consulted the screen. The red dot had suddenly started moving upwards again.

"It's on the move! It must've heard us," he announced.

"Probably your footsteps," said Smithy, as Tabatha tore her hand from his mouth. "I didn't want to say, but you thump around like your shoes are filled with cement."

"It wasn't my footsteps, it was your—"

Before Denzel could finish the sentence, Tabatha grabbed him and dragged him through the door. Sure enough, they emerged into a large, garage-like room lined with dozens of high-tech vehicles.

They were, Denzel thought, some of the sleekest, coolest-looking machines he'd ever seen, and would have been even more so were it not for the fact that most of them were on fire.

"There!" said Tabatha, pointing ahead with her cane. A flowing white figure was dodging through the flaming wreckage, zigzagging across the garage towards a ramp that led to a large roll-up door. Symbols had been etched into the metal, presumably to stop any ghosts from phasing through it.

"Are we sure that's even a ghost?" asked Denzel, as Tabatha set off in pursuit. He and Smithy stumbled along behind her, trying to keep up. "It looks like someone in a white sheet!"

"Scanner says it's a ghost," Tabatha reminded him. "But it doesn't matter. Ghost or not, it's our only lead. If we want to find out what's going on, we need to catch it."

She raised her cane and bellowed, "Stop!" The word bounced around inside the cavernous garage, but the fleeing figure didn't slow.

A bolt of energy streaked from the end of Tabatha's cane. It was a warning shot that sailed harmlessly above the maybe-ghost's head and detonated against the far wall.

The figure weaved suddenly to the right, as if it had spotted some other exit in that direction. Then it scurried across to a row of motorbike-like vehicles that had been toppled over but not, as far as Denzel could tell from this distance, blown to pieces.

"It's going for one of those bikes," Tabatha cried.

Denzel wheezed as he stumbled along behind her. "It's fine. All vehicles are locked down. You can't just jump on and start one."

The ghost jumped on one of the bikes, fiddled with some cables down under the handlebars and fired up the engine.

"Or maybe you can," Denzel groaned.

Tyres screeching, the bike surged forwards and then

skidded towards the ramp. The engine roared, powering it up the slope towards the roll-up door. It weaved from side to side, dodging a couple of Tabatha's cane blasts.

"It can't pass through it," Denzel said. "Those are protection symbols. Ghosts can't phase through anything with—"

There was a deafening *bang* as a missile was launched from the front of the bike and struck the door ahead, punching a hole straight through the metal.

"OK, that was actually pretty awesome," said Tabatha. She made the same sudden right-hand turn as the ghost had and arrived at another of the bikes just as the first one went roaring through the hole in the door.

Grabbing the handlebars of another bike, she stood it up on its wheels. "Get on," she urged, nodding to the seat.

"Who?" asked Smithy and Denzel at the same time. "Him or me?"

"Both of you. Denzel first. You're driving."

"I can't drive!" Denzel protested. "I'm not old enough."

"Doesn't matter," said Tabatha.

"And I've never been on one of these things before!"

"Also doesn't matter."

"And I don't know how to drive!"

"*You'll figure it out!*" Tabatha barked. "The ghost is

getting away. We need to move. Now."

With a groan, Denzel swung his leg over the bike and slid himself towards the front. Something in the seat seemed to grip his bottom, and a series of metal clips locked in place over both legs, pinning them in place.

"I don't like that much," he grumbled.

"Budge up," said Smithy, sliding on behind him. Nothing locked in place around his legs, so he wrapped his arms around Denzel and squeezed so hard Denzel's eyes almost bulged out of his head.

"Not so tight," Denzel spluttered.

Smithy relaxed just enough to allow Denzel to breathe. As he did, Tabatha hoisted up another bike beside them and jumped on. Just like the other ghost had done, she rummaged around under the handlebars and Denzel saw a series of sparks come from the ends of two exposed wires.

"I don't know how to do that," he pointed out.

"You don't need to. You're official," Tabatha said. She let out a little *whoop* as her bike fired up, then twisted the throttle and gunned the engine. "Grab the handlebars."

Denzel tentatively placed his hands on the bike's handlebars. The rubber grip hummed against his skin for a moment, then a heads-up display appeared on the curved screen that stuck up from the bike's front.

Some Japanese writing appeared, followed by his own name in English.

"It says you're an authorised user," Smithy said, then he and Denzel both yelped as Tabatha roared past them towards the ramp.

"Hurry up!" she urged. "Before it gets away!"

Denzel steeled himself. "OK. I can do this," he said.

"You can do this!" Smithy confirmed.

Denzel swallowed. "Here goes."

"You can totally do this!" Smithy cheered.

Denzel twisted the throttle. The bike shot backwards at quite a high speed. They both screamed, then let out a collective "Oof!" when they crashed into the wreckage of a tank-like thing in the row behind them.

"Other way," said Smithy. "Go forward."

"I'm trying to go forward!" Denzel explained. "But I don't know—"

He twisted the controls in the opposite direction. The bike reared up on to its back wheel and lurched forwards in a series of screeching bunny hops.

"Like that, only faster," suggested Smithy. "And use both wheels."

Denzel didn't waste his breath replying. Instead, he eased off on the throttle a little, leaned his weight to the front and brought the front wheel down with a *thump*.

The bike crawled ahead slowly, wobbling like it was about to fall over.

"Maybe you should press that button," said Smithy, pointing past him to a small yellow button on the dash. "It says 'Ride Assist'."

"I think I'm getting the hang of it," Denzel replied.

Smithy looked around as they teetered slowly through the gap in the wreckage where they'd taken the bike from.

After a moment, he reached over and pressed the button.

The display was suddenly filled with streams and streams of Japanese writing, moving too fast for Smithy to be able to translate. For a fraction of a second, Denzel thought he saw the words "He is coming" written in English among all the other text, but then it was gone, and he couldn't be sure he hadn't imagined it.

As he was wondering about this, three other things happened.

A male Japanese voice began booming instructions from a speaker on the front of the bike. Neither boy knew what it was saying, so they both ignored it.

A jet of white-hot flame ignited at the back of the bike. This was harder to ignore, although the thing that happened a fraction of a second later took their mind off it.

The bike moved.

No. That wasn't doing it justice.

The bike went from an almost standing start to what felt like several hundred miles per hour in the space of a couple of seconds. The saddle and leg straps held Denzel in place as the garage became a blur.

There was some screeching, some skidding and a distinct smell of burning rubber as the bike went roaring towards the ramp. It rocketed up the slope, before being launched like a projectile through the hole in the door.

Denzel and Smithy didn't scream this time. Not because they weren't scared, but because they were *too* scared to make a sound. They just stared in mute, bleary-eyed horror as the bike sailed through the air above the roofs of several cars, then smashed unceremoniously on to the other side of the road.

It stopped then, the engines chugging noisily, like it was getting its breath back. The boys both looked up and around them at towering city blocks with colourful neon frontages that stood out against the now fully dark night sky.

The neon signs on the buildings were like a rainbow across the darkness. The glowing reds, greens, oranges and blues shone down over an endless stream of late-night traffic. Taxis, mostly, although there were plenty of other vehicles clogging the streets too. Japanese writing was emblazoned across the signs, although quite what any of them said, Denzel had no idea.

Smithy inhaled deeply through his nose. "Ah," he said a little wistfully. "Paris."

And then the jet of flame erupted from the back of the bike again, a voice barked instructions from the dashboard and Denzel, Smithy and the motorcycle all went rocketing along the street.

CHAPTER 17

Horns blared. Voices shouted. The wind whistled shrilly and urgently, as if warning Denzel and Smithy that they were going too fast.

To be fair, they had already figured that one out for themselves.

Denzel was clutching the handlebars, but didn't for one second believe he had any control over the motorcycle. It seemed to have a mind of its own, and was weaving through the slow-moving traffic where possible, then mounting the pavement whenever the road was too congested to navigate through.

Even though he clearly wasn't in control, Denzel felt

like he had to keep his eyes open. This was not easy. The oncoming wind was doing its best to force them closed, and his instincts were screaming at him not to look at all the many things they might be about to crash into that were coming whizzing towards them.

The bike streaked past them all.

Some oncoming cars.

WHOOOSH!

A few late-night diners sitting at tables outside a restaurant.

VROOOM!

A big plastic squirrel wearing an ice cream cone as a hat.

ZOOOM!

They were all there one moment, and gone the next as the motorcycle powered through the streets, completely ignoring any input from Denzel.

A voice crackled from the speaker on the dash. It took Denzel a moment to realise that it wasn't the same gruff Japanese voice as before, but a girl's voice, speaking in a language he actually understood.

"Where are you guys?" asked Tabatha.

"D-don't know!" Denzel yelped back.

"We just passed a big squirrel," said Smithy, leaning over his friend's shoulder. "With a hat on."

There was a moment of silence.

"Real or fake?" Tabatha asked.

"Fake," Denzel blurted.

Even over all the other sounds, they heard Tabatha exhale. "That's a relief. It's been a weird enough day already."

The bike mounted the pavement and roared through a group of pedestrians, forcing them to jump clear. They shouted furiously and waved their fists in Denzel and Smithy's direction.

"Sorry! Not our fault!" Smithy called back to them.

"What was that?" Tabatha asked.

"N-nothing," said Denzel. "Just another near miss."

"I think I worked out how we can hook up," Tabatha said.

Smithy's head immediately appeared over Denzel's shoulder. He smiled charmingly down at the speaker. "I'm listening..."

"What do you mean?" Denzel asked. He briefly shut his eyes as the bike launched itself back into traffic, then opened them to find the headlights of a truck blaring towards them.

Instinctively, he leaned left, trying to steer the bike that way. It went right instead, narrowly squeaked past the truck, then swung sharply in the opposite direction, cutting in front of a taxi and forcing the driver to slam on the brakes.

"I mean I can remotely connect to your bike and have you come find me," Tabatha said. "I've got the ghost in sight. We can take it down."

Denzel liked the sound of that. Taking a ghost down might not be his favourite way to spend an evening, but he was pretty sure it would mean stopping the bike and getting off – something he was very much in favour of.

"OK. Do that then," he squeaked.

Some Japanese text lit up on the display. "It says you should press there to accept the connection," Smithy explained. He narrowed his eyes and squinted. "Or it might say something about kiwi fruit – it's hard to tell when we're bumping around."

Denzel decided to risk it and touched the screen. The text changed colour then vanished. No kiwi fruits appeared, or at least not to the best of his knowledge.

He wasn't sure what he'd been expecting, really. He'd thought the bike might change direction. He'd hoped it would slow down, but he hadn't been counting on it.

Instead, to his amazement, it sped up.

The neon storefronts, which had been a series of bright blurry shapes, became a single smear of colour. The sounds of the city fell silent, replaced by the howling of the wind and the whining of the engine between Denzel and Smithy's legs.

There was some more screaming, although everything was going too fast for them to figure out which of them it was coming from.

A sudden right turn whipped Smithy's legs straight through the bike. Denzel gasped as Smithy's arms tightened around his stomach, squeezing the air out of him.

"Hold on!" Denzel cried, but the bike was moving so quickly that the words were whipped out of his mouth and sent tumbling along the street behind them.

The bike swerved left. Smithy was jerked back towards the bike, and managed to turn his lower half solid again when he landed in the seat.

"That was unpleasant," he said, then they both launched into another round of screaming when the bike pulled a series of ultra-fast swerves and dodges. Turning sharply, the bike powered down an alleyway so narrow it almost touched the handlebars on both sides, roared out into another street, drawing horn blasts and angry shouts, then slowed suddenly when it pulled up alongside another identical bike.

"Everything all right?" asked Tabatha, looking them up and down. "You both look like you've just seen a ghost."

She looked ahead to where Denzel and Smithy could

just make out another bike dodging through the traffic. "Speaking of which…"

Tabatha's bike weaved on to the pavement and Denzel's motorcycle fell into line behind it.

"Is she steering us?" asked Smithy.

"I think so," said Denzel.

"That's good. At least you don't have to do it," Smithy reasoned.

"It's good if she doesn't crash," Denzel pointed out. "If she does crash, then it's bad."

"Suppose," said Smithy. "Still, on the bright side, I'll be fine."

"How will you be—" Denzel began, before realising what Smithy meant. "Oh, yeah. Ghost."

"Exactamundo."

Another horn blared. It was a deep, booming sort of horn that made Denzel picture a big truck with an angry driver bearing down on him. This, coincidentally, was exactly what was happening, but a sudden burst of acceleration from Tabatha dragged the trailing bike clear. Denzel felt the *whoosh* of the truck's wind as it powered past, and the heat of the driver's furious glare on the back of his head.

Tabatha's voice came from the console speaker. "It's getting away."

SPECTRE COLLECTORS

Denzel narrowed his eyes against the oncoming wind and peered past the bike in front. The target motorcycle was almost at the other end of the street, the high speeds making the sheet-like ghost flap violently.

"Be ready with the scanner," Tabatha instructed. "If it reaches the end of the street and turns, there's no way we'll be able to keep track of it without the scanner."

A cold, clammy feeling of dread descended over Denzel.

The scanner. What had he done with the scanner?

He checked his belt, where it had been clipped for a while.

Nope.

He patted his pockets, taking one hand off the handlebars at a time.

Nothing.

"Do you have the scanner?" he whispered, looking back over his shoulder.

Smithy shook his head. "You had it."

"I know I *had* it," Denzel said. "But I don't have it now."

Tabatha's voice was an urgent bark. "You don't have the scanner?"

Denzel winced. She wasn't supposed to have heard that yet.

"I mean, it might be here somewhere," he said,

checking all the same pockets he'd already checked a moment ago.

"OK, Plan B," said Tabatha. "Smithy, how long can you phase you, Denzel and the bike for?"

Smithy puffed out his chest. "Oh, ages."

"I need more detail than that," Tabatha told him.

Smithy calculated for a moment. "About... All at once, yeah?"

"Yes! All at once!"

"About four seconds."

Denzel spluttered. "How is that *ages*?"

"It's ages longer than you could do it," Smithy pointed out.

Denzel couldn't really argue with that. Even if he wanted to, there wasn't time, as Tabatha's bike immediately turned and sped towards a towering building, dragging Denzel and Smithy along behind.

"Wall," Denzel mumbled, nodding ahead of them. "Wall. There's a wall. Big wall."

"Smithy, get ready," Tabatha said.

"Wall!" Denzel yelped, on the off-chance that no one else had noticed the huge building looming dead ahead. "Watch out for the—"

Tabatha and her bike phased through the wall. Denzel heard Smithy give a little grunt of effort and felt the arms around him pull tighter.

As the wall rushed up to meet them, Denzel instinctively closed his eyes and screamed a number of rude words.

And then, with a *whoosh*, they were through the wall, solid again, and powering across the plush foyer of an expensive-looking hotel, tyres chewing up the carpet.

A lot of people shouted a lot of things at them in Japanese. Denzel guessed that these were probably rude words too.

Tabatha's bike smashed through some high-backed leather armchairs, shattered a couple of glass coffee tables and then zoomed past the reception desk.

Denzel held on to his handlebars, his cheeks burning, his eyes staring straight ahead as he tried to ignore the chaos around them.

"Sorry," he mumbled, before Smithy tightened his grip again and they passed through another wall like a ghost. Or, more accurately, like a ghost, his best friend, and the motorbike they were both riding on.

Car horns blasted. More people shouted. In the distance, a police siren wailed.

And then there was another wall ahead of them, and Tabatha showed no sign of slowing down.

Denzel tried not to close his eyes this time, but his brain became increasingly insistent as they sped towards the building. A few seconds before they reached it, his instincts won out, and when he next opened his eyes he saw Tabatha's bike carving a trench through a fast-food restaurant, scattering tables and knocking aside chairs.

There was a lot of screaming, some more shouting, a chorus of bangs, breaks and smashes, and then they were through another wall and into the building next door.

This one was another restaurant, although it looked more high-class than the previous one. At least, it looked more high-class when they arrived. By the time two motorbikes had torn through it, it wasn't quite as impressive.

They passed through three more restaurants, two karaoke bars and a small comedy club where everyone whooped and cheered them as they thundered across the stage, mistaking them for part of the act.

"Wow, this is tiring," Smithy groaned.

"Almost there! Hang on!" Tabatha replied via the intercom.

And then, with a sudden burst of speed, both bikes plunged through a final wall and out into another busy street lit by garish neon signs.

"Brace yourself!" Tabatha warned.

For a split second, Denzel and Smithy caught a glimpse

of something white and flappy dead ahead of Tabatha's bike.

There was a *bang*. There was a *crash*.

And then Tabatha's motorcycle and the bike they had been chasing became a tangle of metal bouncing and rolling across the road.

Cars swerved to avoid the bikes and found each other instead. Brakes screeched and tyres spun as multiple vehicles tried to avoid smashing into those ahead, but failed.

Denzel and Smithy's own bike came to a sudden stop, and they both sat there wincing as vehicles collided all around them.

Smithy leaned forwards in the seat so his face was next to Denzel's. "You *do* have insurance, right?" he asked.

Denzel slowly shook his head.

"Oh. That's unfortunate," Smithy said, leaning back.

The restraints that had been holding Denzel's legs in place unclipped themselves. He jumped off in case they tried to trap him again.

Across the street, Tabatha sprang out of the wreckage, spun round and pointed with her cane to where a figure in a white sheet was making a run for it.

"What are you just standing there for?" she barked. "It's getting away!"

CHAPTER 18

Denzel had never been a big fan of running. It required a lot of effort, hurt his knees and was generally an unpleasant experience that he did his best to avoid.

Recently he'd found himself running quite a lot. Usually he was running away from things. This was much easier than normal running, because no matter how unpleasant running was, it was better than being torn apart by ghosts and monsters.

Now, though, he was chasing something that might be a ghost or monster, and he was finding this type of running even harder than usual. He was still wearing the ugly necklace Mrs Gourlay had given him, and the weight of it pulled the chain tight against the back of his neck with every step.

The problem, he thought, wasn't just that his legs were hurting and his breath was short. It was more the fact that he wasn't sure he wanted to actually catch the thing they were chasing.

What if it tried to eat him?

Or worse, what if it *did* eat him?

He was about to offer a compelling argument for why they shouldn't be chasing a ghost through the streets of Tokyo when the ghost in question phased through the ornate stone frontage of what looked like an old theatre building and vanished inside. A couple of nearby pedestrians gave little gasps of surprise, but most people just walked on with their heads down, eyes fixed on the pavement ahead.

Tabatha, who had been leading the chase, caught Denzel by the left wrist and Smithy grabbed on to Denzel's right, the three of them forming a ghost-human-ghost chain as they raced towards the theatre.

As ever, Denzel took a deep breath right before they plunged through the wall, afraid that he might accidentally inhale a brick on the way through.

They stumbled into the grand but faded foyer of an old Japanese theatre that had seen better days. The theatre looked to be closed, although a couple of lights had been left on, presumably for security purposes.

The general impression Denzel got of the place involved a lot of red curtains and gargoyle-like faces carved out of solid gold. On closer inspection, though, he saw that the gold was just paint, and that much of it was peeling away in flakes.

A series of grimacing white-painted faces leered out at them from posters on the wall. For a moment, one of the faces seemed to be moving, then Denzel realised he was watching the flowing white ghost pass through the poster.

"There!" he said, against his better judgement.

He braced himself again as Tabatha dragged him and Smithy into a lumbering run. The poster they were racing towards showed a close-up of a man wearing white and red make-up. His mouth was wide open, either shouting or singing, and Denzel couldn't shake the feeling that he was being swallowed whole when Tabatha pulled him through the poster and the wall behind it.

They emerged into some sort of backstage area, filled with painted trees, some garishly coloured costumes on hangers, and several tables that held nothing but ornate paper fans.

Tabatha's shout was short and sharp. "Freeze, or I'll shoot!"

The figure in white didn't freeze. Instead, it ducked behind a fake tree, which immediately lost several cardboard branches when Tabatha shot it with a blast from her cane.

"Tiiimbeeeer!" Smithy shouted.

Denzel caught a glimpse of the ghost hiding behind the smoking remains of the scenery, then it dropped through the floor as if a trapdoor had opened directly below it.

He began to sink the moment Tabatha grabbed his hand. They fell through the floorboards and into a dark, dingy basement below. It had the same low-level security lighting as everywhere else in the theatre, so Denzel got a half-decent view of the concrete floor several metres below him, right before he smashed into it.

"Ow! Bit of warning next time would be nice!" he hissed, quickly patting himself down to make sure nothing was broken.

Tabatha had already sprung to her feet, and now stood with her cane pointed at the ghost they had been chasing.

"Make one more move and you're ectoplasm!" she warned.

The ghost had its back to them, but stood perfectly still. Then, very slowly, it raised its hands.

"Wait, were we chasing someone?" asked Smithy.

Denzel side-eyed him as he got to his feet. "Yes. Of course. Why do you think we were racing about like that?"

Smithy shrugged. "I thought it was just, you know, for a laugh."

"For a *laugh*? But... But..." Denzel shook his head and sighed. "Doesn't matter."

Up close, Denzel could see that the ghost wasn't covered by a sheet at all. Instead, it wore something that looked like a hoodie crossed with a cape. The material was fluffy and warm-looking, with two long rabbit-like ears stitched on to the top of the hood.

"Did we just capture Bugs Bunny?" Smithy whispered.

"Turn round," Tabatha ordered.

Smithy turned round.

"Not you," said Denzel.

Smithy turned back.

To begin with, the ghost didn't move, but then it clearly thought better of ignoring the only person in the room wielding a weapon, and slowly shuffled around on the spot.

As the ghost turned, it pushed down its hood, revealing

a crop of bright-pink hair and two of the largest eyes Denzel had ever seen. Considering he'd once been very close to the front end of a giant shark, this was really saying something.

Her irises were the same pink colour as her hair, which should have been horrifying but actually looked pretty nice.

Both eyes shimmered, reflecting at least three different light sources that Denzel was pretty sure didn't exist in this room. One of the light sources appeared to be heart-shaped.

Under her hoodie-cape, she wore a skirt that was the precise same pink as her eyes and hair, and a white T-shirt with a picture of an overweight unicorn on it, and too many rainbows to count.

She reminded Denzel less of a real person and more like someone from a Japanese video game or anime cartoon. When she spoke, he expected it to be in Japanese, and was pleasantly surprised when her words came out in slightly broken English.

"Please, no shoot! No shoot!"

"Don't give me a reason to," Tabatha replied, but she kept her cane raised, the little hand on the end making a gun-like motion with one finger and thumb. "Who are you? Why did you run? What were you doing in that underground complex?"

"What happened to the Spectre Collectors?" Denzel asked, adding to the growing list of questions.

"Where did you get that cape?" demanded Smithy. "I like the ears."

"Saku. Saku," babbled the ghost girl, prodding herself right on the cartoon unicorn. "I am Saku."

She frowned in concentration, as if struggling to find the right words. "I ... woke up in that place. I do not remember how I was there. But, when I woke, there was ... much noise."

She cupped her hands near her ears and shook them. "Very scary."

"What kind of noise?" asked Denzel.

"Big noise. Bad noise," Saku whispered. "Very scary."

Her huge eyes darted left and right, as if checking to see if the coast was clear. "And crazy as this will sound, there were ghosts."

Denzel and Smithy exchanged glances. "What do you mean?" Denzel asked.

"Ghosts," Saku repeated. She held her hands in front of her and made a wailing sound. "Wooooo! Ghosts. Yes? You have heard of ghosts?"

"Once or twice," said Smithy.

"Very scary," Saku said again. She shivered, as if cold.

"Very scary ghosts. I no like that. No like ghosts."

Denzel's face was a picture of confusion. He opened his mouth and raised a finger as if to speak, thought about it some more, then finally voiced the words the others were almost certainly thinking.

Well, maybe not Smithy.

"But ... you *are* a ghost."

Saku's big eyes somehow grew larger. Her mouth, which was half the size of one eye at most, dropped open.

"Pardon?"

"Well, I mean, you're a ghost, aren't you?" said Denzel. "You ran through walls. You phased through the floor. You're a ghost."

Saku stared blankly back at him.

"She is, isn't she?" Denzel asked Tabatha, just in case it was him who had got the wrong end of the stick. "She is a ghost?"

Tabatha nodded. "Sure is."

"Right. Right," said Denzel, glad he'd had this confirmed.

Saku shook her head. "No. No, not ghost!"

"It's OK, it's OK," said Smithy, raising his hands in a soothing gesture. "I'm a ghost too. And so's she."

He and Tabatha both smiled broadly at Saku. She

stared at them both in turn for a while, head tick-tocking between them.

And then she screamed.

It was quite a shrill, high-pitched scream, and only ended when Tabatha slapped her across the face with the little golden hand on the end of her cane.

"Pull yourself together," Tabatha told her. "You're a ghost, we're both ghosts, deal with it. Tell us what you know. What happened to the others back at the complex? Where is everyone?"

Saku's eyes shimmered like she was about to burst into tears, but then she sniffed, whispered something to herself in Japanese and straightened. "Men were there. Men in robes. There was much fighting. Battles. Explosions. Boom! They wanted 'Chosen One'. That's what they say. 'Give us Chosen One! Where is Chosen One?'"

Denzel shifted uncomfortably on his feet but said nothing.

"They say Chosen One key to lock. Chosen One open everything. Chosen One *important* to them." Her voice dropped into another whisper. "To one they call 'Ghostfather'."

"And did they find this Chosen One?" asked Tabatha, deliberately not so much as glancing in Denzel's direction.

"Oh, yes!" said Saku, nodding enthusiastically. "Yes!"

"They did?" asked Denzel. "Are you sure?"

"Yes! Lured the Chosen One out, they did. Drew him away."

It was Smithy's turn to frown. "Hold on, hold on," he said, turning in Denzel's direction. "I thought *you* were—"

"Shh," said Tabatha, shooting him a warning glare over her shoulder. It was, Smithy thought, the most beautiful warning glare he'd ever had shot at him, and he sighed happily as he did what he was told and stopped talking.

When Tabatha turned back, there was something different about Saku. She had pulled up her hood, half-covering her pink hair.

Saku continued speaking, but while her accent was unchanged, she had suddenly become much more fluent in the English language. The words flowed out without thought or hesitation.

"It was easy enough. Show up on a scanner, make a run for it, always staying just far enough ahead for you to keep up, but not close enough that you smell a rat. I couldn't make it too easy for you, or you'd see right through it."

As she spoke, the ears on her hood twitched excitedly. "Of course, now that I meet you face to face, I can see you're not bright enough to see through anything."

"Oh look, the ears move! How cool is that?" said Smithy, completely failing to pick up on the change of atmosphere in the room. "I'm totally getting a hoodie like that before we go home."

"You had us chase you deliberately," said Tabatha. "You wanted us to follow you. Why?"

Saku shrugged. "Nothing personal, honest," she said, smiling sweetly. "It was just business."

From the shadowy corners of the basement came the *shinkt* of swords being drawn. Six Samurai-ghosts stepped into view, blades raised and ready to start swinging. Behind them, several figures in long robes shuffled out of the darkness, Ghostfather symbols emblazoned on their chests.

"I'd drop the cane," Saku told Tabatha. "These guys are crazy fast."

Tabatha looked around at the other occupants of the room, spent a few seconds calculating her chances, then let her cane fall to the floor.

"Very sensible," Saku told her.

A cloth bag landed on the floor at Saku's feet. It *chinked* in a way that made Denzel think of gold coins and pirate chests.

"You have done well, Saku," intoned one of the hooded

figures. "We shall call on your services again someday."

"Any time, boss," said Saku, taking the bag and hooking it on to her belt.

She gave a little giggle and smiled at Denzel and the others. Then she raised two fingers in a peace sign, winked at no one in particular and went streaking upwards through the ceiling above.

"Well," said Smithy after a moment's pause. "She seemed nice."

CHAPTER 19

Denzel didn't remember being knocked out. He guessed he must've been at some point, though, because the next thing he knew, he was waking up.

It was not, he quickly concluded, the nicest way he'd ever woken up.

He was strapped to some sort of rack at the top of a flight of wide stone steps, his arms and legs spread in an X-shape and secured across the wrists and ankles with lengths of gold-coloured rope not unlike the belts the Oberon Spectre Collectors wore.

He was dressed in a bright-yellow robe, the hood of which had been pulled up and secured with another piece of rope across his forehead.

Worrying as all this was, it was actually quite far down the list of the things that were currently concerning him. Highlights of this list included:

The hundreds of robed figures all gathered around holding candles. They were definitely on the list.

The dozens of Samurai-ghosts standing guard around him, one hand on the hilt of their sheathed swords. They made the list too.

The fact they were all assembled in what looked like some sort of underground tomb, with arcane symbols adorning the walls, floor and ceiling.

The sacrificial altar that stood in the middle of the floor, dark-red stains marking the stone. That was pretty high up, although not quite at the top of the list.

Currently sitting in the number-one spot on Denzel's list of concerns was the enormous curved guillotine blade that hung above him, positioned so that if it fell it would slice him neatly into two halves – specifically, a front half and a back half.

Denzel really didn't want to be chopped in half. And, if he was going to be, those were probably the last two halves he'd choose. Top and bottom would've been better. Left side and right side, at a push. But front and back? That felt like someone was trying extra hard to be mean.

There was some chanting going on, Denzel realised. It was coming from the hooded figures, but he couldn't understand it and it didn't sound very friendly, so he decided it was probably best not to dwell on it too much. It wasn't like he didn't already have a literal list of worrying things to dwell on, after all.

A figure in a purple robe stood by the altar, waving his arms around as if conducting the chants. Denzel wasn't sure this was the same person they'd met back in Scotland, but the robe and height matched pretty closely, so he assumed it was.

Not that it really mattered. If he was going to be chopped in half and sacrificed, he wasn't all that fussed about being on first-name terms with the person who did it.

Denzel couldn't see Smithy or Tabatha anywhere. With a bit of luck, they'd escaped and were planning a dramatic last-minute rescue, but luck had never really been Denzel's strong point.

Despite everything that was going on, and his growing list of concerns, Denzel felt oddly calm about it all. Sure, he was terrified, but he wasn't *panicking* for some reason. Maybe he was just getting braver. Maybe he was finally becoming a real Spectre Collector.

Or maybe it was something to do with the soothing smell that rose like smoke from all those candles, and the way the chanting was numbing his brain.

Probably those last ones, he decided.

He realised that he hadn't yet shouted or screamed, and felt he should probably address this as a matter of urgency. He'd used up his lifetime's screaming quota on the back of the motorbike, he reckoned, so he decided he'd shout something.

Denzel spent a few seconds trying to come up with something dramatic and cool to shout, but couldn't think of anything. Instead, he yelled, "Hey!" in quite a half-hearted way, and everyone completely ignored him.

He decided to try getting free of the ropes that bound him to the frame. The ropes didn't look too thick, and he reckoned if he really went for it he could work at least one hand free. After that, getting the rest of himself out would be child's play, and he could leg it as fast as he could towards the stone staircase at the far end of the tomb.

Denzel really went for it.

Four seconds later, he stopped really going for it and accepted that there was absolutely no hope of him breaking free.

During those four seconds, the chanting stopped.

Denzel didn't notice this until after he'd stopped really going for it with the ropes, and by the time he'd stopped his brief-but-frantic thrashing, the last traces of the final "Ommm" were echoing into silence.

As one, every hood in the room angled upwards in his direction. The Samurai-ghosts continued to face front, hands on their sword hilts. It would be nice to think that they were there for his protection, Denzel thought, but he knew they would really be there to stop anyone trying to rescue him.

The silence felt heavy and oppressive. Denzel felt an overwhelming urge to fill it.

"Hello," he said.

He wasn't sure why he said "Hello". Of all the things he could have said, given his current circumstances, "Hello" didn't feel particularly appropriate.

He tried again.

"You'd better let me go," he warned. "I am a Spectre Collector in the Seventh Army of the Enlightened, a … a…" His mouth went dry. "A Messenger of the Allwhere. A soldier in the Seventh Army of… Wait, no, I've done that one."

"Silence," said the figure in purple.

Denzel was almost grateful for the opportunity to stop talking. It hadn't been going very well for him.

A very low-level chanting resumed as the cult leader pushed back his hood to reveal a head so old and withered-looking Denzel's first thought was that the man was a zombie.

Technically, his first thought was "Ew!" but the zombie thing was a close second.

His wrinkled skin was tattooed with dozens of symbols, all connected by a series of twisting lines. He looked like someone had printed a map of the London Underground on a walnut, then brought it to life.

"Welcome, Chosen One," the cult leader said. "I am the Shakarath."

"We meet at last," said Denzel. Again, he felt that this was quite an odd thing to say, given the situation, but it just slipped out on its own. He blamed the candle fumes.

The Shakarath hesitated. "Yes. Well, we've already met, but … OK."

"Or have we?" asked Denzel.

"Yes. Yes, we have. In Scotland," said the Shakarath. He gestured to his robe. "I was wearing this."

"Or *were* you?" asked Denzel.

The Shakarath's ravaged features frowned for a moment, then he turned and gestured to the other hooded figures. On cue, they all blew out their candles.

The smell faded quickly and Denzel felt his veins

filling with icy-cold terror. It didn't help that, now that the candles were out, the tomb was substantially darker than it had been a few moments before.

A few torches hung from brackets on the ancient walls, their flickering flames sending shadows scurrying and scrabbling across the masonry. The shadows deepened the crags in the Shakarath's face, somehow making him look even worse.

"Do you know why you are here?" the old man asked.

The last of the candle fumes were still working their way through Denzel's brain, which was probably why he said what he said.

"Are you throwing me a surprise party?" he asked. "Is it my birthday?"

The Shakarath smiled grimly. "You know, in a way, it is," he said. The menacing way in which he said it cleared Denzel's head of the final traces of the fumes.

Now thinking clearly again, Denzel felt the panic really start to set in. He swallowed hard, trying to keep his terror from exploding out of him in a scream.

He wanted to cry. Well, he didn't *want* to cry – crying was the last thing he wanted to do – but he could feel a good cry bubbling up inside him. He bit firmly on his tongue and held the tears back through sheer force of will. There was no way he was going to cry in front of this lot.

Wetting himself was a real possibility, but crying? Never.

"You are here because we brought you here," said the Shakarath. Even in his growing panic, Denzel felt this was a pretty obvious statement, but he decided not to mention it. "We have been leading you here for quite some time now, Chosen One. We have been planning this moment since long before you were born."

He gestured around with a hand that was almost as withered as his head. "This. All this was built for you. Centuries ago. Built for this day. For this moment. For this great thing we are about to do."

He raised his voice and Denzel got the impression the cult leader was no longer talking to him.

"For the return of the Ghostfather!"

Denzel remembered the feeling of standing on the hillside in that vision he'd had back in Mrs Gourlay's house. He remembered the oceans boiling and the land burning. He remembered the screams, the pain, the destruction.

He remembered the end of the world.

"My friends will stop you," he said. "They'll come for me."

The Shakarath raised a crooked finger, as if he'd just

remembered something. "Oh. Wait."

He rummaged inside the baggy sleeves of his robe and then produced two large red gemstones like the ones the Spectre Collectors used to trap ghosts. They were both wrapped in thin lengths of willow branches, binding the spirits inside.

"You mean these friends?"

He raised both gems so they were closer to his mouth. "Are you coming to rescue him? Hmm? Are you? Are you?" he asked, in the sort of voice usually reserved for talking to babies or excited dogs.

Turning his head, he listened to the gems, then shrugged.

"Doesn't sound like it," he said, then he shook both gems violently before tossing them on to the sacrificial altar. "Pathetic," he sneered. "Traitors to their own kind. The Ghostfather himself shall choose their punishments. History tells us He can be most ... creative."

The Shakarath clasped his hands in front of himself and emerged from behind the altar. He appeared to glide across the floor until he reached the bottom of the steps that led up to Denzel, but came no further.

"You do not realise how special you are, Chosen One," he said. "When the signs told us of your birth, we acted quickly to take you from your natural parents and hide you, so that none may interfere with our plans."

Denzel felt his stomach twist into one giant knot. The tears threatened to come again, and he had to work hard to force them back.

"Wait, what are you saying? My adoptive parents knew about this? My dads worked for you?"

The Shakarath made a dismissive gesture. "Those idiots? Of course not. They had no idea. We chose them at random. They were desperate to adopt a child, and we knew they would keep you safe until you were ready."

A single tear made it past Denzel's defences. Despite the awfulness of his situation, it was a tear of happiness and relief. His dads weren't in on any of it. They weren't actors playing a role. They weren't undercover agents for an ancient cult. They were just his dads.

If he was going to die, he'd at least die knowing that.

"And now, finally, you *are* ready," the cult leader said.

"Ready for what?" Denzel demanded, his voice rising into a shout. "I still don't know what you need me for."

Something malicious twinkled in the Shakarath's eyes. "Then perhaps it is time for you to find out," he said. He raised a hand above his head, fist clenched. "Prepare the Key!"

Four of the hooded figures broke ranks and walked forward, each drawing a long, curved piece of pointy metal from their sleeves.

Denzel didn't know what they were going to do with those bits of metal, exactly, but he was pretty sure it was nothing he was going to enjoy. He struggled against his ropes, kicking and thrashing as he tried desperately to break free.

"Let me go! Let me go! You're making a mistake! I'm not the key!" he cried. "I'm not the key!"

The Shakarath snorted out something that was not unlike a laugh. "The Key? Of course you're not the Key!"

He gestured to the sacrificial altar, where the four hooded figures were slotting the bits of metal together.

"This is the Key, Chosen One."

Denzel blinked in surprise. "Uh. Right," he said. "What? I thought...?"

"You are not the Key, boy. You never were," said the Shakarath. His puckered mouth twisted into a grin, showing a set of brown teeth. "You are the prison. You are the lock."

His voice became a scratchy hiss as, all around the tomb, the chanting resumed.

"The Ghostfather resides in you. And tonight, we're breaking Him out."

CHAPTER 20

Denzel had questions. He had a lot of questions. He had so many questions, in fact, that he couldn't decide which one to ask first.

He eventually settled on, "Huh?"

"It is detailed in the historical records. In the *Book of Lum*," said the Shakarath. The way he said it reminded Denzel of one of his old teachers telling him off for not doing his homework. "Lum tells us that a thousand thousand lifetimes from the banishing of the Ghostfather, He shall be reborn anew through the vessel of a child."

"But – but how do you know it's me?" asked Denzel.

"We guessed," said the Shakarath.

"You *guessed*?"

"No, we used magic, you fool. Our greatest scholars and mages have been searching for you for generations. The very moment that you were born, the entire world's Spectral Energy levels went up by four bings."

Denzel didn't know if four bings was a lot of bings or not. The way the cult leader said it suggested it probably was.

"When we found you, one of our mages attempted to link with your then infant mind," the Shakarath continued. "He exploded. We knew then that we had found the Chosen One, and our plans were quickly put in place."

"You stole me from my parents," Denzel said. He'd been aware of this since the Shakarath had first told him, of course, but he'd had a lot on his mind, and it was only really sinking in now. He steeled himself for the answer to his next question. "What did you do with them?"

"The exploding wizard I mentioned?" said the Shakarath, raising a wispy grey eyebrow. "Your parents were standing next to him at the time."

For the first time since he'd woken up in the tomb, Denzel was grateful to be strapped to the rack, otherwise he'd have fallen down.

Life with his dads had been pretty much perfect, but

he'd occasionally wondered about his real parents, and what had happened to them. Being blown to bits by an evil ghost cult had not been a possibility he had considered.

"Those children – your Spectre Collectors – thought you were special. Thought you had power of your own. Little did they realise that the biggest, most powerful ghost in history was lurking within you," said the Shakarath. "Without the Ghostfather, you would be nothing, boy."

Denzel would've quite liked to have been nothing, if it meant not having his parents blown up and not being strapped in an X-shape about to be sacrificed by a mad cult, but he was too shaken to say any of it.

Instead, he asked the most pressing question he had. It came out as a low, frightened croak.

"What happens now?"

The Shakarath stepped aside, revealing that the four cultists had assembled their device on the altar. It stood beside the two red gemstones their leader had tossed there earlier, and Denzel found himself worrying about the fates of Smithy and Tabatha as much as his own.

"Now?" said the Shakarath, excitement building on his withered face. "Now, we begin."

He thrust both hands into the air and the low, murmured chanting rose until it became a series of rhythmic grunts and shouts. Every single robed figure in the room, the Shakarath included, began an elaborate series of hand gestures and turns, moving in perfect harmony.

It reminded him of the time his dads had taken him line-dancing at the community centre, only no one here was wearing a cowboy hat, and it was much less embarrassing in general. Still, he'd have taken line-dancing any day over his current predicament, which was really saying something.

The device the cultists had put together – the Key – glowed a faint green colour. From this angle, Denzel couldn't tell if the pointy bit at the front was aimed at him or at the huge blade hanging above him. He wasn't sure what would be worse – being blasted open or sliced in half. Neither one was ideal.

He began to shout and scream, to thrash against his restraints.

"Help!" he shouted. Desperately. Hopelessly. "Someone help!"

His eyes went to the door up the staircase at the far end of the tomb, longing to see Samara and Boyle come charging through. He'd take Rasmus and Knightley if he had to. In fact, at this particular moment, he'd be happy to see any random stranger come strolling through the door, as long they weren't wearing a big robe or carrying a Samurai sword.

The door remained closed though.

No one was coming.

The chanting rose in both passion and volume, becoming something that wouldn't have sounded out of place at a football match.

The Key *hummed*, then glowed so bright Denzel could no longer look at it without it hurting his eyes.

On some secret cue, the chanting stopped. Its echo explored the cavernous tomb for a few seconds, then faded into silence.

The Shakarath whispered a single word in a language Denzel didn't understand.

And then a beam of magical energy fired from the end of the Key, and all Denzel knew was pain.

CHAPTER 21

He could feel him. Even through the pain and the fear, Denzel could feel the Ghostfather stirring somewhere inside him. It started as a fluttering in his stomach, then a rumbling like an earthquake in his brain.

And then, he knew. He knew the Shakarath wasn't crazy. Well, he probably was crazy, but he was also right.

The Ghostfather was inside Denzel. And it was time for him to come out.

A feeling of weightlessness washed over Denzel. He experienced the same *whooshing* sensation he felt whenever Smithy pulled him through a wall, and then he was on his hands and knees on the floor, having phased through the restraints that had been holding him in place.

The whining of the Key stopped. Its glow faded, and the tomb was plunged back into shadowy torchlight.

Denzel's fingers stretched out and then curved back in like claws. He watched them flex in and out, in and out against the rough stone floor, fully aware that he was not the one making them move.

Gritting his teeth, he forced his hands to behave themselves. They trembled in protest, but the fingers stopped flexing. Denzel could feel the urge building up in them though, like water behind a dam.

He gasped when the truth dawned on him. The Ghostfather wasn't going to come bursting out of him. The Ghostfather was *becoming* him. He was taking over Denzel's body to use for his own.

Denzel managed to raise his head to look at the Shakarath and all the other cultists. They watched him in breathless silence, and Denzel could actually feel the excitement rising from them in waves.

Even the Samurai-ghosts had turned to look at him now. Their hands no longer gripped the hilts of their swords. Presumably, there was no longer any danger of anyone messing up the ceremony. The damage was already done.

But Denzel could still do some damage of his own.

His legs refused to obey him at first, so he let his fingers go back to flexing and focused all his willpower on his feet.

The right one moved first, kicking him up into a clumsy, lumbering stagger down the stone staircase. The left leg wasn't as keen to get involved and he fell the final few steps, rolled clumsily at the bottom and hit his head on the floor with a *crack*.

The impact seemed to stun the Ghostfather more than it did him, and Denzel's muscles were suddenly back under his control. The cultists and Samurai-ghosts backed away from him as he lurched over to the sacrificial altar.

"The Key! Give me the Key!" Denzel cried. As he did, the pitch of his voice rose and fell, fluctuating between a scratchy yelp and a deep drone.

He *thudded* against the front of the altar. Directly across the other side of it, the Shakarath's puckered mouth twisted into a smirk.

"The Key won't help you now. Nothing will help you now."

"Didn't really want the Key anyway," Denzel wheezed. He grabbed for the gemstones containing Smithy and

Tabatha, but the old man was much faster than he looked.

The Shakarath's zombie-like hands snatched the gems up before Denzel could get to them.

"Now now," the cult leader said. "Let's not do anything silly."

"Give them to me," Denzel pleaded.

"It's too late, boy."

"Give them to me!"

"Your friends are gone. And soon, you shall be too."

"GIVE THEM TO ME!"

The third time Denzel said the words, he didn't think it was really him saying them at all. The voice seemed to erupt from inside him, a deep, booming bass drum of rage.

As it did, the Shakarath moved backwards. It took Denzel a moment to realise that he was not retreating of his own free will, and had instead been propelled backwards at quite a high speed.

In the spot where he had been standing, both gemstones floated in mid-air. Denzel felt a near-overwhelming urge to eat them both, to absorb their ghostly contents into himself and boost his growing power.

Fortunately, he was able to resist. With some effort,

he forced his hands to pluck the gemstones from the air.

Meanwhile, several dozen metres across the room, the Shakarath *crunched* against the stone steps. He lay there groaning as Denzel convinced his shaking fingers to unwind the lengths of willow from around each gem.

Two of the Samurai-ghosts came up behind him, swords drawn. Denzel wasn't sure how he knew this, exactly, because he hadn't turned around. It was like he could see them in his head, every detail crisp and clear in his mind's eye.

He vaporised them with a thought.

No, not him. It wasn't *him*, he told himself. It was the Ghostfather. The Ghostfather had destroyed them. The Ghostfather would destroy them all.

"You i-idiots," he said, struggling to make his lips form the words. "You h-have n-n-no idea what you've d-done."

The power inside him was growing, and as it did, he got a better sense of who the Ghostfather was. He had no loyalty to this cult. He had no loyalty to anyone. If he took control, he would kill them all in a heartbeat. And then the world would be next.

Denzel had planned to throw the gems to the floor, but there was no need for that now. He was strong enough to just clench his fists around them and crush them both into powder.

As the gemstones shattered, Smithy and Tabatha came tumbling out. Tabatha landed in a crouch, already twirling her cane. Smithy hit the floor with an "Oof!" then pulled himself upright, made a series of karate-chopping gestures at the world in general, and whooped with excitement when he saw his best friend.

"Denzel! You're alive! Nice robe. Very few people can successfully wear bright yellow, but on you it works."

His face fell.

"Wow, you look terrible," he said. "You're all sweaty. Why are you so sweaty? You look like a pig in a sauna."

Denzel nodded shakily.

"And your face is all..." Smithy contorted his face into an angry snarl. "Like that. And a bit..." He puffed out his cheeks. "A bit that."

Denzel managed another nod.

"And why are you doing that with your fingers? And why's your hair standing on end? And why are you floating?"

Denzel looked down. Sure enough, he was levitating a few centimetres off the ground. That was new, and yet he wasn't actually all that surprised.

"I'm th-the Ghostfather," Denzel managed to say.

Tabatha spun on the spot, her eyebrows arching in surprise.

"Are you?" said Smithy. "Wow. That's crazy. You look just like my mate Denzel." He glanced around. "Have you seen him?"

"That is Denzel," Tabatha said.

Smithy shook his head. "That's what I thought, but he reckons he's the Ghostfather. I mean, it's an easy mistake to make, the resemblance is uncanny."

"He's Denzel *and* he's the Ghostfather," Tabatha clarified.

Smithy looked Denzel up and down. "Oh. Right." He frowned. "How does that work?"

"N-not very w-well," Denzel slurred. "H-help me."

"I should have seen this," Tabatha said, staring deep into Denzel's eyes. "Of course he's inside you. It's the perfect hiding place."

Four of the Samurai-ghosts moved to attack. Tabatha blasted one with her cane, while Denzel obliterated the others with a wave of his hand.

The Ghostfather's power and rage were both building, but he could still direct them, at least. He could still keep his friends safe.

Even, he realised, if he couldn't save himself.

"You h-have to go," he said. "G-get out."

"We're not leaving you," said Smithy, turning serious.

"You have to," Denzel hissed. He suddenly found

himself disliking Smithy. He disliked his stupid face. He hated his inane chatter. He despised everything about him.

"No!" Denzel roared, driving the thoughts away. His voice became a series of breathless sobs. "C-can't control it m-much longer. P-please, Smithy. Go. Just go."

The air around Denzel crackled and hummed. Little electrical charges flickered across his skin. Pain tore up his insides and he gasped, blowing out two of the torches on the other side of the tomb.

The cultists, who had all seemed right behind the whole *bring back the Ghostfather* thing until now, started shifting uneasily on their feet. A couple of them looked over to where the Shakarath lay groaning on the steps, then past him to the door beyond, sizing up their chances of escape.

Denzel noticed none of this. He was too preoccupied by the icy-cold fingers that came creeping into his brain. At first he wanted to scream, but then his head was filled with seductive thoughts of power.

"So ... strong," he whispered, his eyes turning glassy and dark. "So powerful. He can do anything. *I* can do anything. The world will be ours. His. Mine. All shall crumble before us. All shall fall."

"OK, that doesn't sound good," said Tabatha. "Denzel?

Denzel, can you hear me?"

Denzel blinked. Sweat poured down his forehead, but his arms ignored his instructions to wipe his face on his sleeve.

"Go," he whispered. "P-please, just go."

"I have an idea," said Tabatha. "But it's insane."

"I'm in," said Smithy.

"Like *really* insane."

"I'm even more in," Smithy replied. "What do we do?"

Tabatha caught Smithy by the hand. He stared at it for a moment, blushed, but said nothing.

"Have you ever possessed anyone before?" she asked him.

"Um, once or twice," Smithy admitted. He crinkled his nose. "It didn't end well."

"Third time's the charm," said Tabatha. She drew herself up to her full height. "Ready?"

Denzel felt his anger boiling up inside him. What were these two insignificant insects babbling about? He should consume them. Devour them whole.

"Ready," said Smithy. He also drew himself up to his full height, but his full height wasn't all that much, so it wasn't very impressive.

"Wh-what are you d-doing?" Denzel demanded.

"Ready, steady..." Tabatha said.

Both ghosts jumped at the same time, throwing themselves towards Denzel.

"Possess!" Smithy yelped, then Denzel staggered as he felt them both phase into him.

For several seconds Denzel felt like his brain was being smashed by hammers and kicked around the floor, as he and three other people all tried to exist in the same body at the same time.

And then he heard a voice. Or maybe felt it; he wasn't sure. Whichever, the effect was the same.

He laughed. Despite every terrible thing currently going on, he laughed.

"Dark in here, innit?" said Smithy.

"Budge up," said Tabatha.

"I shall flay your flesh from your very bones!" said the Ghostfather, which sort of killed the mood a bit.

Denzel could still feel the Ghostfather raging inside him, but it was easier to resist him now that he had back-up. His power was still growing though, and Denzel knew it was only a matter of time before he became too strong for even the three of them to contain.

"OK, here's what we're going to do," said Tabatha. "This is the insane bit I mentioned."

"Wait, this *wasn't* the crazy part?" Denzel said. He was the only one actually speaking out loud, much to the confusion of the cultists. Many of them had started edging their way to the door now, no doubt reconsidering some of their recent life choices.

"No. This was actually pretty sensible compared to what happens next," said Tabatha.

"Do we make Denzel pick his nose and eat it?" asked Smithy.

"What? Ew. No," said Tabatha.

"I will destroy you! I will destroy all!" raged the Ghostfather.

Everyone ignored him.

"There's only one way we're getting rid of this guy," said Tabatha. "We have to open a portal to the Spectral Realm."

CHAPTER 22

Denzel let out a little yelp of terror. He had some experience of portals into the Spectral Realm, and he didn't really want to get involved with another one.

"What? No! We can't do that! We've seen one of those and they're not good! It'll gobble up everything in the room. It'll destroy everything!"

That was the straw that broke the cultists' backs. They turned as one, hitched up their robes and began legging it up the stairs, completely ignoring the semi-conscious Shakarath who lay spread-eagled on the staircase beside them.

"It's the only way," Tabatha told Denzel. "We use the

Ghostfather's power to open a portal and we trap him inside."

"Quick question," said Smithy. "Won't that mean we're trapped inside too? Like, all of us?"

Tabatha shook her head. Denzel wasn't sure how he knew this, exactly, but he did.

"No, we can jump out at the last minute."

"That's it? That's your escape plan?" Denzel asked. *"Jump out at the last minute?"*

"Denzel can't jump out!" Smithy pointed out. "He'll get pulled in along with the Ghostfather."

"It's ... it's fine," Denzel said, quickly coming to the conclusion that they didn't have many other options open to them. "She's right. It's the only way to stop him. I can feel it. He's too powerful. He'll destroy everything." He took a deep breath. "I'll do it. I'll sacrifice myself."

"Actually, you don't have to," said Tabatha.

Denzel let out a huge sigh of relief. "Oh, thank God."

"You see, we haven't actually possessed you, Denzel."

"You haven't?"

"We haven't?" echoed Smithy.

"We've possessed the Ghostfather," Tabatha explained.

They all felt the Ghostfather writhe angrily at this suggestion, as if he were taking offence.

"So? What's the difference?" Denzel asked.

"The difference is that we can do this."

She made a sound like someone straining to lift something heavy. Denzel felt a sudden sensation of movement, like a hand had pushed him in the middle of the chest. He stumbled and fell to the floor, and found himself staring up at a figure carved from darkness itself.

The air around it warped and buckled, as if the figure's very existence was bending reality.

"Foolish children."

The words were the Ghostfather's, Denzel knew, but he couldn't pinpoint exactly where they'd come from.

"You cannot hope to stop me. I am the Alpha and the Omega, the beginning and the end, the first and the last. I am the destructor of all things. I am the Ghost—"

There was a *parp* as the Ghostfather loudly broke wind.

"Sorry," said Smithy, his voice coming from somewhere around the Ghostfather's middle. "That was me."

"How ... how *dare* you?" boomed the Ghostfather.

"You ready, Smithy?" asked Tabatha.

"Not really," Smithy confirmed. "But I'll give it a go."

"Then let's do it!"

The Ghostfather's arms raised jerkily. Energy crackled from his fingertips, turning his midnight-black digits into flickering shades of electric blue. The space behind Denzel creaked and groaned as reality was pulled aside like a pair of curtains.

Scrambling for cover behind the altar, Denzel gazed into the swirling vortex of colours and shapes that was the Spectral Realm. As he watched, some of the shapes took form, becoming things that were almost, but not *quite*, as frightening as the Ghostfather himself.

Denzel heard a wind whistling through the tomb, but couldn't feel it. The Ghostfather clearly could though. His feet began to slide on the floor as the portal pulled him closer.

"N-no! Not again!" he wailed. "Not again!"

"OK, Smithy, time to abandon ship," said Tabatha. "Three, two, one, go!"

Tabatha came rolling out from inside the Ghostfather's towering frame. Smithy, however, did not.

"Smithy?" said Denzel. "Smithy, what are you doing?"

"He's ... he's so strong," said Smithy, and at first Denzel thought his friend couldn't break free. He quickly realised that this wasn't the problem though.

"So much power. I can use it all," Smithy continued. "I can see it all. I can see everything. How it works. How it's all connected. I can see everything that has ever happened. I can do *anything*."

"What you're going to want to do is get out of there," Tabatha said. The Ghostfather's feet carved little trenches in the stone floor as he was dragged towards the swirling portal. "Hurry! Before it's too late!"

"Just coming," said Smithy. "There's something I want to do first."

"Smithy, hurry!" Denzel cried. "Whatever it is, it's not important. Get out!"

"It *is* important," said Smithy. "It's very important."

The Ghostfather's body fell forwards and hit the floor. Now off-balance, it began to slide faster and faster in the direction of the portal.

"It isn't more important than you, Smithy! Please, get out!" Denzel hollered.

"You're running out of time, kid!" Tabatha added. "Get out of there and you can take me to the cinema."

"Almost ... done it..." said Smithy.

"No time," warned Tabatha. She ran at the Ghostfather's thrashing body, dived towards it and phased cleanly through it. When she came rolling out, she was clutching a limp and frail-looking Smithy in her arms.

Tabatha kicked them both away from the portal just as the Ghostfather tumbled the last few metres towards it. His fingers dug frantically into the ground, slowing him down, but it wasn't enough. With a *whoosh*, he was sucked inside, and went tumbling into the swirling abyss of colour beyond.

"We did it!" said Denzel, rushing to where Tabatha was laying Smithy on the floor. "Guys, we did it! We got rid of him!"

Smithy smiled weakly and gave a thumbs-up. "Nice one."

"What were you thinking, you idiot?" Tabatha demanded. "You could've been stuck in there with him!"

"It was important," wheezed Smithy. He grinned goofily. "So ... the cinema?"

Tabatha scowled for a moment, then sighed. "Fine," she said. "But nothing romantic. Something violent."

"Deal," said Smithy. "There's this great one with a woman in it. It's based on a true story."

Tabatha frowned. "That's a bit vague."

"He means *King Kong*," said Denzel. "I know, I know. Don't ask. Long story."

Denzel turned, smiling with relief at a job well done. They'd stopped the Ghostfather. They'd saved the world. Somehow despite all the odds, they'd—

"Um, guys," said Denzel.

The others looked up at him.

"Should the portal still be open?"

The others considered this for a moment.

"Ideally not," said Tabatha.

She and Smithy got to their feet. The hole in reality was widening slowly, growing a centimetre or two every second. Inside the dancing vortex of colours, they could see the shape of the Ghostfather. He had stopped tumbling now, and was standing upright, energy crackling across his body.

"Is it just me, or is he getting bigger?" asked Smithy. "It's like he's absorbing the energy."

"He's either getting bigger or closer," said Denzel. Neither of these options struck him as being very good. "How do we close it?"

Tabatha rubbed her tongue against the front of her teeth for a while as she thought this through. "We, uh... Well, I mean, we..." She shrugged. "I have no idea."

"What do you mean you have no idea?!" Denzel yelped. "It was your idea to open it!"

"And that was a great idea," said Tabatha. "Truly a first-class plan. I think we can all agree on that."

"Yep," said Smithy.

Denzel was too terrified to reply, and just gestured in the direction of the portal, using nothing but body language to argue that no, it wasn't a first-class plan, actually. It was a terrible plan.

"All we need now is a second plan," said Tabatha. "The first plan was a success, and now we just need a second plan to tidy up the loose ends."

Denzel didn't think an ancient evil ghost absorbing the power of the Spectral Realm could really be classed as "loose ends" but he ignored that and concentrated on more pressing matters.

"So what's the second plan?"

"I don't know yet," Tabatha admitted. "I came up with the first plan – I was kind of hoping one of you guys would come up with the second."

Smithy clicked his fingers. "I've got it!"

All eyes turned his way.

"We shut the portal to the Spectral Realm!" he said. Grinning proudly, he tucked his thumbs into a pair of imaginary braces and leaned back, looking very pleased with himself indeed. "I thank you."

Denzel blinked several times. "No. But... I mean, yes... I mean, obviously that's what we have to do. But *how* do we do it?"

Smithy's grin fell a little, but not all the way. "Well, it seems to me like Tabatha and I have *both* come up with great plans, Denzel. I think it's only fair that you figure out the last bit."

"Yours wasn't even a plan!" Denzel protested, but

there was no time to argue.

The Ghostfather was definitely getting larger, and definitely getting closer too. He approached with slow, lumbering footsteps, his shiny black body awash with all the colours of the rainbow, and several others that hadn't made the cut.

Denzel's mind raced. He estimated he had maybe a minute until the Ghostfather was big enough and large enough to reach through the portal. One minute to stop him. One minute to save the world.

"Magic," Denzel said. "We need magic. That's how they closed it before."

"I know a few tricks, but nothing that could close this thing," said Tabatha.

"I know one brilliant trick," said Smithy. "Does anyone have a watch, or a piece of jewellery on them? Preferably one they don't mind losing, because I haven't actually managed to get the trick to work before."

"Not that sort of magic!" Denzel told him. "I meant proper magic like—"

He stopped.

Piece of jewellery.

Follow the Ghostfather.

Scrabbling at the hideous yellow robe, Denzel frantically pulled it open, revealing his bare chest below.

He'd hoped to find the pendant there, but no such luck. It must have been taken by the cultists.

Spinning on his heel, Denzel saw the Shakarath crawling slowly up the stairs at the other end of the tomb. Vaulting the altar, he broke into a run, his bare feet *thumping* on the floor as he closed in on the old man.

"Where is it?" he demanded, stumbling to a stop beside the Shakarath. "Where's the necklace?"

"You'll never find it," the Shakarath hissed. "I've hidden it in the last place you'd ever think to—"

Denzel fished in the pocket of the old man's robe. "Got it!"

The Shakarath sighed and slumped on to the steps as Denzel turned back to the portal. He almost screamed when he saw how close and how enormous the Ghostfather was now. He'd be through any second, and there'd be no hope of stopping him then.

The necklace *hummed* in Denzel's hand. As he held it by the chain, the pendant rose to point in the direction of the portal, as if being pulled in.

"Follow the Ghostfather," Denzel whispered, then he released his grip and watched as the pendant went rocketing across the room.

As it flew, it seemed to grow. By the time it passed

the event horizon, it was five times as big as when it had started.

By the time it *thwacked* the Ghostfather between the eyes, it was the size of a tractor tyre.

As the Ghostfather reeled from the impact, the edges of the portal began knitting together. The howling wind died as the hole in reality sealed shut.

Just before it did, a furious roar echoed around the tomb, but then was cut off as the portal ceased to exist.

For a long time, there was nothing but silence, and then Smithy finally broke it.

"And *stay* out."

There was a sudden commotion from the doorway up the stairs behind Denzel. He turned, raising his fists, bracing himself for a sea of angry cult members to come rushing in.

Instead he was met by two very familiar faces.

"There you are!" barked Boyle, as he and Samara came racing down the steps. Several more Spectre Collectors appeared through the doorway behind him, many of them Japanese. "We were worried sick!"

Boyle checked himself. "Samara. Samara was worried sick," he corrected.

Denzel flopped down on to the steps, exhausted but happy. It was over. It was finally over.

"Anything exciting happen before we arrived?" asked Samara.

Denzel glanced over to Tabatha and Smithy and smiled. "Nah," he said. "Nothing we couldn't handle."

CHAPTER 23

Denzel and Smithy sat in the back of a van, with Boyle and Samara in the seats up front. It was the same van the boys had first been bundled into all those weeks before, when they'd thought they were being kidnapped.

Back then, Denzel hadn't even known that Smithy was a ghost. It was amazing how much his life had changed in such a short space of time.

The trip back from Japan had been much quicker than the trip there. It had involved several teleportation hops though, so Denzel wasn't sure which journey he'd preferred. Given the choice, he'd probably have walked back home.

When they'd returned, there had been a big debriefing, where Denzel, Smithy and Tabatha had explained everything that had happened. The Japanese Spectre Collectors had connected via some big floating-head magic thing that Denzel didn't really understand, and informed them that all the cultists had been rounded up.

Denzel had been worried that the Japanese chapter of the organisation might all have been horribly killed, but it turned out that they'd just been locked in their own dining hall, with enchantments placed on the doors to stop them breaking out.

Once the Japanese delegate's massive floating head had left, conversation turned to the subject of recapturing all the ghosts who had been let out of containment. Boyle and Samara had told Denzel they'd need his help for that, which was when Denzel had dropped the bombshell.

"I don't think I can," he'd said. This had earned him some confused looks from the other Spectre Collectors present. "I don't think it was me seeing the ghosts in the first place. I think that was the Ghostfather."

A test was arranged. One of the few remaining gems was brought up to the meeting room. It contained a poltergeist like the one Denzel had first seen in his house way back at the start.

They'd set it free from its gemstone prison. Denzel had looked around the room for a while, trying to see the same smoky octopus shape he'd seen before.

But no. Nothing. His power had gone.

After the poltergeist had spent the next five minutes tossing things around the room before Boyle finally caught it, the meeting had been called to a close. Smithy had asked to speak to Samara and Boyle privately, and when they'd emerged ten minutes later, all three of them had looked ... weird. Not happy, but not sad either. Or both, maybe, at the same time.

And now Denzel and Smithy were in the back of the van on a quiet street across town from Spectre Collectors HQ.

"So what's the plan?" asked Denzel. "What are we doing? Is it a ghost thing?"

He shook his head. "What am I saying? Of course it's a ghost thing. It's always a ghost thing."

He smiled at Smithy, but Smithy didn't meet his eye.

"What's the matter? What's wrong?" Denzel asked.

Boyle was facing front, looking ahead at the street. Samara was half turned in her chair but she wasn't meeting Denzel's gaze either.

"What's going on?" Denzel asked.

"I did something," said Smithy. "When I was in the

Ghostfather. I did something."

Denzel frowned. "What did you do?"

"I wasn't sure it would work, but we checked, and... It worked," Smithy continued. "It worked."

"What worked?" Denzel asked. "What are you on about?"

"You were the best friend I ever had, Denzel," said Smithy. "Dead or alive."

"You're my best friend too," Denzel began, then his brain processed what Smithy had said. "Wait, what do you mean, 'were'?"

He patted himself down. "Oh God, did I die? Am I dead?"

Smithy smiled sadly. "No. You're not dead. I wish you were."

"Oh, thanks a lot!" Denzel said.

"Then we could hang out all the time," Smithy quickly added.

"We hang out all the time now," Denzel pointed out.

Smithy gave a small nod and an even smaller sigh. "I'll never forget you, Denzel," he said, his voice cracking.

The van doors opened on to a street that Denzel knew all too well. "What is this? What's happening?" he demanded, turning to Samara and Boyle.

He saw the dust in Samara's hand a fraction of a

second before she blew on it. He tried to hold his breath, but only succeeded in inhaling a large quantity of the dust in one big gulp.

"Goodbye, Denzel," he heard Smithy whisper. "I'll miss you."

Denzel frowned and looked around him. He was standing on the pavement. Was that right? How long had he been standing there for? He couldn't remember. Was this where he was supposed to be?

He had a niggling feeling that it wasn't, and that he'd been somewhere else very recently, but he couldn't remember where. He watched a white van driving away up the street and the niggle grew more insistent for a moment.

He tried to focus on it, but the front door of a house opened across the road and he lost his concentration. Two men appeared and waved to him.

"Denzel. There you are," said his parents, beckoning him in. "Come on, we've ordered Chinese."

The niggle in Denzel's brain stopped, and all doubt left him. This was right. This was where he was meant to be.

"Coming, Dads," he said.

And then, Denzel Edgar hurried across the road, up his garden path and finally returned home.

EPILOGUE

Denzel sat on a low wall around the back of the school, eating a thick sandwich from an overflowing lunch box. He'd always liked this spot. It was quiet. Peaceful, even.

Sure, the bin beside the wall absolutely stank, but at least he was out of the way of the older kids here, and less likely to get himself beaten up for looking at someone the wrong way.

He was just about to start on the second half of the sandwich when a scruffy-looking shorter kid appeared beside him, startling him.

"Where did you come from?" Denzel asked, looking the boy up and down. He'd never seen him before, and yet there was something about his dishevelled appearance that seemed familiar.

"Around," said the other kid.

He hopped up on to the wall beside Denzel, produced a scrunched-up paper bag from his pocket and then tentatively looked inside.

"You going to eat that?" he asked, eyeing up Denzel's sandwich.

"I was, yeah," Denzel confirmed.

"Want to swap?" the boy asked, holding up his paper bag. Denzel regarded it warily.

"What have you got?"

"Egg."

"What kind of egg?"

"Just egg."

Denzel shook his head. "No, you're all right."

He held his lunchbox out. "You can have that chocolate though."

"Nice one. Thanks!"

The boy took the chocolate bar from the box.

"It's vegan though," Denzel warned.

The boy replaced the chocolate bar in the box.

They sat in silence for a while. Denzel wasn't used to having anyone sit round here with him and yet it didn't feel unnatural. It felt ... right, somehow.

"Here, what would you rather, right?" asked the new kid.

"Go on."

"Have all these amazing, mind-blowing things happen to you, but never be able to remember them," the boy said. "Or never have anything amazing happen to you at all?"

Denzel chewed his sandwich while he considered this.

"First one, probably," he said.

The new kid smiled. It was a big, broad, goofy sort of smile that made Denzel want to laugh.

"I hoped you'd say that," the boy said, holding out a hand. "I'm Smithy," he said. "And I reckon this could be the start of a beautiful friendship..."